MARILYN DENNY THOMAS

Arrivederci, Y'all!

SISTERS TOGETHER FOREVER
in italy

FURROW
PRESS

Arrivederci, Y'all!
Sisters Together Forever in Italy
Copyright © 2011 by Marilyn Denny Thomas
Published by Furrow Press
P.O. Box 98
Big Flats, New York 14814-0098
www.furrowpress.com

Edited by Edie Mourey

Cover and interior design by David G. Danglis
Photo of Venice: © iStockPhoto/iSailorr
Photo of flag: © iStockPhoto/CGinspiration

Printed in the United States of America.
Library of Congress Control Number: 2011933198
International Standard Book Number: 978-0-9800196-9-8

Other Books by Marilyn Denny Thomas

The Gentile and the Jew: A Divine Romance

Going Home: A Divine Journey

Sweet Beulah Land

Dan and Jeannie: Their Story (e-book)

Acknowledgments

YEAR AFTER YEAR, my husband, Ricky Thomas, makes the top of my thankful list. He supports my writing with love, patience and understanding. This time he even moved our lives around a bit to give me more time and space to write. Thank you, my husband and my best friend.

My two lovely daughters, Joelle Thomas and Jodi Fucili, are my favorite fans. Thank you as always for giving hours of your life to proofreading. And thank you, girls, for all your love and support as well as the sweet pride you have in your mother.

A big thank-you goes to our office manager, Peggy Rhodes, for taking over many of my office responsibilities so that I could hide away and write. You're the best, Peg.

Edie Mourey, my delightful editor and friend has now become my publisher as well. Thank you, Edie, for the time and expertise you made so readily available 24/7. I look forward to many more years of delightful ventures.

A big thank you to Dave Danglis, the book's cover and interior designer, who went beyond the call of duty and found issues all the proofreaders missed!

Very special thanks go to my dear friend, Beverlie Brewer, who read the manuscript of *Arrivederci, Y'all!* as I wrote it, page by page, offering skilled advice and stimulating ideas as well as loads of encouragement. Beverlie also proofread for hours on end and helped with cover ideas as well. Thanks a million, BB!

Dedication

This book was inspired by six lovely women
whose friendships have sustained me for many years.
We have laughed and cried together, prayed and played together,
and supported one another through thick and thin.
My deepest thanks to the real-life Lyn, Annie, Diana, Christmas,
Jules and Suzanne. To you, I dedicate this book.

Preface

WHO AM I AND WHAT DO I HAVE TO DO with this delightful group of seven women and their now historical adventure? I'll tell you. I am the seventh, the one who almost didn't get to go. That's another story, of course, but one that I might possibly tell at some point; not because it might interest you but because my story is my sisters' story as well, not to mention that I am the world's best meanderer of rabbit trails.

You must remember throughout this saga that we are *Seven*. It's much more than a number, you know. Somewhere back in my mind's file cabinet is a folder called, "High School Highlights." I won't take time to name all the folders in that cabinet because it might take forever; that is, if I can remember them all which I probably can't. Anyway, when I think about seven being more than a physical number, I quickly retrieve this little scientific nugget from one of those files: *The whole is greater than the sum of its parts.* It makes my point perfectly.

Now that the journey is over and we are home safe and sound, I'm trying as best I can to tell our story on paper just in case anyone is interested. I've listened intently to Jules's description of the perfect journey, Christmas's list of her new friends, Diana's word sketches of the lovely Italian landscapes and Annie's *hmms*. Suzanne? Being her first trip to Italy, and just because she is who she is, Suzanne came back with notebooks filled with journaling and memos she jotted down at each and every place we visited, including the prison where St. Paul was entombed. Jules tried to dance in the tiny dark pit. Annie squinted her eyes in thought, and Christmas stood in the corner with a contented smile on her face. Suzanne shined her keychain flashlight on a sheet of paper she had stuck in her pocket and took notes. No wonder we designated her to be the official scribe. You probably think I've forgotten Lyn, but I haven't. She didn't have much to say about the apostle Paul's prison cell or anything else. Every time I tried to pull some thoughts out of her, she just shook her head and cried. But I'm getting ahead of myself. Sorry about that. I'll try to tell this tale from memory and just as it was related to me by the others, the facts made possible only because of Suzanne's sheer determination to take excellent notes.

Marnie

Chapter One

THE AIRPORT ATMOSPHERE was like the State Fair in Raleigh on a Saturday night; it was packed, wild and crazy, everyone looking around like they had no idea where to go next. And Suzanne and Jules didn't—know where to go, that is.

Three hours back, while Diana coordinated the stopover in Montreal, very calmly giving our little covey of seven female travelers instructions on where and what time to meet, Suzanne and Jules had eyed a little shop across the corridor with colorful Indian saris in the window. Almost before Diana uttered her last word, the two scurried over to the New Delhi Boutique. Suzanne told me later that she and Jules were just too excited to sit around and wait so they roamed from shop to shop with a few snack bars in between. Now they wished they had listened to Diana's instructions.

Nevertheless, the two youngest of our group were not concerned. Somewhere in the bottomless abyss of Jules's purse rested their boarding passes. Suzanne—a very soft-spoken, English teacher—said she was pretty sure she remembered Diana saying they were to meet at Gate E, but it might be best to fish out the tickets and take a look just in case. Jules vaguely recalled something about three hours, but she wasn't positive either, so they revved up seldom used speed and darted in and out of the masses, arriving at Gate E panting and laughing to beat the band.

Of course, we five waiting travelers had become terribly anxious and had grown more so by the minute. The plane was already loading, and the line wasn't very long. Per our usual, though, we took one look at the prodigals' laughing faces, and with a symphony of sighs, we shook our heads and joined the fun.

"Here, girls, hand me your shopping bags and get your boarding passes out quick," said Christmas. (To her friends it seemed she was appropriately named, seeing she sprinkled a bit of the beneficent spirit everywhere she went.)

Jules had stuffed the passes back down in the abyss, the very same way she crammed so many activities in the small space of her life. She taught advanced placement chemistry, raised goats, led adult and children's dance teams and rode a horse named Jason for fifteen years. Sad to say, Jason died this past year, but fortunately, a new horse came her way and then two more, Miles and Luna. Not a horse person myself, I was, however, terribly impressed to learn that Miles and Luna were descendants of the magnificent Secretariat. After all, I did see the movie, and who wouldn't be a little awed by such celebrity status?

"Come on!" I grabbed my carry-on case and rushed through the entrance to the loading ramp. "Better hurry. We can't miss this flight, or we'll miss Rome altogether!"

"There's no way I'm going to go home and tell Pops I spent the night in the Montreal airport and then turned around and flew back home," laughed Lyn. "It's been a miracle to get this far." She handed the attendant her boarding pass and hurried to catch up with Annie who was marching up the ramp with deliberate steps, keeping rank with the travelers in front of her.

Annie was the oldest and the most mature. She had the ability to look as if there was never a rush, even in emergencies. Diana was close behind, trying to remember who made that famous statement about the well laid plans of mice and men. Christmas patiently held the shopping bags.

Just as the attendant's patience was beginning to wear thin, Jules exclaimed, "Here they are!"

Spinning around like a ballerina on a music box, she whirled over to the attendant. Suzanne followed close behind, relief written all over her face.

"Wait, Jules!" shouted Christmas. "You left your carry-on!"

The fuming attendant's mouth flew open, but she held her wrath in check, and by the time Jules handed her the boarding pass with a smiling, "I'm so sorry," her anger took flight. She flashed the daunting customer a quick smile in return.

"Thank you for flying Air Canada," she said.

Suzanne rather doubted the genuineness of her statement, but Jules happily replied, "You're very welcome!"

The good-looking pilot and two flight attendants were getting ready to tighten the hatches when they spotted three more travelers hurrying up the ramp, pushing and pulling and laughing.

"Hold it!" said the pilot to his helpers. "Welcome aboard, ladies!"

"Oh, thank you! So sorry we're late," huffed Jules, dazzling the pilot with her pearly whites. "Oh, no! Suzanne! I left our saris somewhere."

"I have them, safe and sound," replied Christmas calmly. She smiled sweetly and greeted the Asian attendant in fluent Japanese. The young woman was absolutely thrilled. Never in a million years would she have suspected the five-foot-nine sandy blonde American wearing a size nine shoe would speak Japanese. Christmas agreed to meet Makiko at the beverage counter sometime during the six-hour flight and tell the girl about her buddy, a Japanese ventriloquist dummy named Ken Chan, KC for short.

Thankfully, the overnight flight was not filled to capacity. We had purchased our tickets early so we had three seats in the center aisle and another four seats right behind those. Diana, the elected coordinator of our journey because of her previous trips to Italy, had chosen that particular seating arrangement because it allowed us to talk and keep together. It proved even better than she thought because a few seats were empty and we gals—ranging in age from fifty to sixty-five—could take turns stretching out from time to time.

After a bit of excited chatter about the trip to Italy—a first for all but Diana—the two-hour drive to Raleigh-Durham Airport, and the connecting flight to Montreal, all the energy-depleting events of the day began to take their toll. Diana was especially tired. As a successful real estate broker and developer of most anything that needed developing, just preparing to be away from the office for two weeks had been exhausting. She put on her elegant sleeping mask while Suzanne and I retrieved the books we were reading from our bags under the seats.

In no time, Suzanne was glued to Rick Steves's guide to Italy, and I was deep into a mystery about copper scrolls and temple treasures in relation to the Vatican. Jules yawned a time or two and quickly drifted off to sleep. I'm sure she was dreaming of dancing through the streets of Rome and browsing its marketplaces where all sorts and colors of silk fabrics and flowing dresses are sold.

When Christmas said goodnight with a little giggle and a glint of mischief in her eyes, Annie replied, "Hmm." She was deep in thought. Annie is Diana's business partner, the steady one who couldn't help but go over the past few days in her mind to make sure she had left nothing undone.

Lyn prayed for Pops—lost without her at home—and for the airplane's engines, the pilots, and all of the trains and taxis the group would ride throughout the entire trip. More than anything, she prayed that no one would get lost. Getting lost was her greatest fear.

It was a long night, but thankfully we seven rested fairly well—except for multiple trips to the restroom. During one of those treks, Christmas was fortunate enough to rendezvous with the Asian flight attendant. By the time the plane landed in Rome the following day and Makiko bid her *yoi ryōko o* or bon voyage as we know it, our friendly Texan had accomplished her usual goal. She now had another lifetime e-mail friend and so did Ken Chan, the dummy.

Seven bedraggled, boggle-eyed women slowly emerged from the gigantic aircraft and hurried as best we could down the ramp to escape being trampled by the passengers behind us. The corridor seemed to be a mile long, but Christmas, with her long legs and quick gait, led us into the brightly lit terminal in no time at all.

"Grab some coffee if you want to," she said, turning back to speak to our droopy crowd. "I'll go on to baggage claim and start gathering our luggage." With that, Christmas was off like a streak of lightning.

"Wait! I'll help you!" shouted Lyn. "I can't drink caffeine anymore because of my blood pressure, and decaf is like drinking bad water. You'll need more help if our bags come down the chute all at once. I'll come with you."

"Me, too!" I hurried to catch up with Lyn. To tell the truth, I had much rather have propped my swollen ankles up in an out-of-the-way corner somewhere, but I have wrestled with an inborn sense of guilt my entire life, and that one little weakness has kept me hopping at times when I should have been stopping. Furthermore, I have a soft spot in my heart for Lyn who has worked hard all her life with very few breaks. It was only right for me to traipse after her.

Noting mine and Lyn's obvious deteriorating physical and mental states, Christmas looked as if she wasn't so sure we'd be much help to her at all. She must have wondered if we would even make it to baggage claim. But we were determined women, the entire bunch actually. So like a duck with two handicapped ducklings in tow, Christmas again headed off to get the luggage while Diana spotted a Starbucks with funny Italian words under the logo. Suzanne espied the coffee shop, too, and quickly gained a new sense of destiny and the energy to get there. To Diana, the several yards looked like Mount Everest.

Jules perked up as well and rushed off after Suzanne shouting, "Take a rest, girls! We'll get your coffee!"

"Tea for me!" yelled Diana at the same time Annie said, "Don't forget the cream!" They sat down on the closest bench and took turns catching their breath.

"We're in Italy . . . finally," said Diana, exhaling the last bit of air in her lungs.

"Finally. But I'm not sure my entire body has arrived as yet." Annie reached down to rub the calf of her leg.

"Yeah, I know."

"How's your foot?"

"My foot?"

"Mhmm, the one you broke last spring?" It was obvious Annie was genuinely concerned.

"Well, it's the part of my anatomy I'd rub if could bend," replied Diana with a wry grin.

"It will be worth it all in the end. This trip is going to be more than we ever imagined."

Diana nodded. If Annie felt that strongly about something, there was little doubt her prediction would come to pass. We sometimes call her E. F. Hutton because when Annie speaks, everyone listens.

Jules and Suzanne came ambling back with two trays of steaming tea and coffee. Noting the curving path of the fairly short journey, Diana wondered if the coffee might be of the Irish persuasion.

"Okay, girls, let's go," said Suzanne.

Diana was too tired to administrate at this point, so Suzanne easily took up the slack. "Maybe the other girls have dragged off the luggage by now," she whispered to Annie.

Annie smiled and said, "Hmm." It meant, "I hope so, too."

In the meantime, Lyn and I dragged quite a ways behind Christmas. Calm as usual but a little frustrated, our tall Texan looked back and motioned that she was going on ahead and would meet us at baggage claim.

By this time, Suzanne and Jules had caught up to Lyn and me.

"I have to go to the restroom, do you?" Jules's green eyes darted up and down the corridor.

Lyn was one tired woman. She plopped down on a nearby bench. "No, I went just before we landed. I'll wait for y'all right here on this bench. Now, don't get lost, you hear?"

"Don't worry. We'll be right back." And with that Jules and Suzanne rushed towards the restroom sign down and across the wide corridor with me close behind. All the while I was concerned that Lyn might fall off the bench before our return, so I kept looking back which slowed me up a bit.

Before I could reach Jules and Suzanne, I spied a man in a frayed jacket and a red beret a couple of yards away. I gasped and froze at the same time. My mind raced, scanning my gray matter's file cabinets like a computer search.

That's Lucien d' Corsa!

I love his art. The man is a modern-day Impressionist, close to Monet and Renoir in my opinion. My dilemma was how to keep him in sight and go to the restroom at the same time. Fortunately, the man seemed to be headed toward the restroom area as well. Being a rather short little sixtyish lady with dark unruly hair, I rushed after him, never thinking what I would do if I caught the guy. Normally, I'm not an impulsive person. Compulsive maybe, but not impulsive. But this time I took off like The Road Runner after Wile E. Coyote. Or was it the other way around? I can't remember now.

"You're in the @#$% wrong room, lady!"

Actually, I didn't know that's what he said until a moment later when an Englishman, who was washing his hands, interpreted the sentence for me. He didn't smile, just rolled his eyes and mumbled, "Americans."

"Oh, no!" My hands instantly flew to cover my eyes as I shrieked, "Is this the men's room?"

The English guy dried his hands, and while the artist ripped off a few more expletives in Italian, he replied dryly, "Yes, my dear, you are now in the men's room of Rome's Leonardo da Vinci Airport. I'm sure this will be bloody exciting to write home about."

"But I was just following Lucien d' Corsa." My hands still covered my eyes.

"Lucien d' Corsa?" asked the Englishman.

"Yes." I pointed to the fuming man in the red beret with one hand and kept the other over my eyes. "He's a famous Italian artist, and I wanted to meet him and let him know how much I admire his work." To tell the truth, I was on the verge of tears, but I still held hope that the Englishman would translate for me and I would get to meet d' Corsa after all. I was also thinking that perhaps d' Corsa's business card was adorned with one of his paintings and he would give me one.

The Englishman switched easily to Italian once more. "Are you Lucien d' Corsa?" he asked the tall man in the red beret who continued to stare at me as though I were his worst enemy or perhaps his uninvited mother-in-law.

D' Corsa answered by shouting something that sounded even more negative and harsh to my Southern ears.

"He says he is most definitely *not* Lucien d' Corsa, lady. Frankly, he hates d' Corsa's work."

I then turned to stare up at the man—alias, Lucien d' Corsa—just as intensely as he was staring at me. "Well, it should be a law that no two people can look that much alike." And then I spun around and zipped out of the men's room.

En route, I heard the Englishman and the Italian speaking in their respective languages, "Americans!"

I ran smack dab into Lyn. "What were you doing in the men's room?" Her green eyes were big as saucers.

"Don't ask!" A few yards down the wide corridor, I changed my mind. "Oh, I'll tell you. I always tell you everything." It was a known fact that Lyn was the best secret keeper in the South.

"I was chasing this artist, you see . . . ." All the way to baggage claim, I explained the harrowing experience to Lyn who, as always, didn't laugh but showed compassion for me in kind expressions and words of sympathy. Actually, I have thought quite often during our lifetime together that Lyn defines friendship.

Five very lovely but worn-out women were standing off to one side of the baggage carousel, luggage piled all around them. I'm sure Lyn and I looked just as bad as or worse than they did. Jules and Suzanne, normally the late ones, had arrived quite a while ago. No one was smiling. Suzanne was the only one who spoke. "Should we ask what happened to you?" Had I not known Suzanne like a book, a hint of sarcasm would have made it to my ear.

"No, I think not. But I want you all to know that it was my fault, not Lyn's. She never gets into . . . well, anyway, it was my fault, and I apologize."

"No, it wasn't anybody's fault," came Lyn to my rescue. "We're accidentally late, and that's all there is to it."

Lyn was known to tell the honest-to-goodness truth with no amplification, so the exhausted women took her word for it and began to gather up the bags. "We're ready now. I'll go tell the cabbie," said Suzanne.

Chapter Two

OUR LITTLE COMPANY OF WEARY TRAVELERS fitted perfectly into a large taxi waiting for us. Within a few minutes after going through customs, we were groggily riding through the Italian countryside and various suburbs, going up to the center of Rome, the ancient city built on seven hills. Having made the journey before, Diana laid her head back on the seat, hoping to take a quick nap before the city center came into view. Suzanne took the time to catch up on her notes. Jules, tucked away in the middle seat, happily watched for the grand structures of old Rome to appear. Lyn, sitting next to the window, pressed her face against the glass, watching, waiting and weeping. She was the one who had a strong aversion to leaving home, and there she was—on foreign soil for the first time in her life. It was a strange feeling, I'm sure.

The Italian driver—happy to have seven well-dressed Americans with nice fat purses in his vehicle—excitedly exclaimed in broken English . . . evidently, one of the few English phrases he knew, "Where to?"

"The Barroco near the Trevi Fountain," said Diana. The driver, nodding his head up and down in affirmation, seemed to repeat the name of the hotel, but we couldn't really tell. All eyes turned toward Diana who said, "*Si*," to the driver and then closed hers. Apparently, all was well.

Lyn, however, could not bring herself to close her eyes and leave the group's welfare to a total stranger in a foreign land—a stranger who couldn't speak our language, at that! She could just picture Aubrey Joe Williams, our hometown police chief, giving Pops the word that his wife had been kidnapped by the Italian Mafia and was being held for ransom in an undisclosed cave somewhere in Sicily. Then she began to wonder how much she was worth. She told me later that, when her mind scanned the last bank statement, she figured there was no way Pops could get her back with the exorbitant ransom money kidnappers required these days.

Tears spilled down her cheeks once more, some at the thought of never seeing Pops and her children again and others rooted in the overwhelming sense of excitement she had felt since the plane landed. The tears, as well as their roots, were all tangled up. She was an emotional mess. Struggling to hold back sobs, Lyn reached over Suzanne to get a tissue from her bag.

She quickly pushed aside her personal problems. "What's wrong, Suzanne?" There was no reply.

"Suzanne!" Lyn gently shook her friend's shoulder.

Most everyone was taking a snooze, but Jules was wide awake in the seat ahead. She turned around. "What's wrong?"

"I don't know. Suzanne started looking really weird, and she hasn't answered me. I guess she could be asleep with her eyes open."

"No, she's not asleep." Jules was worried. "I don't like the looks of this."

Considering that Jules was usually one of the most positive thinking of our group, Lyn's worry thermometer rose a full ten degrees.

Suddenly, Suzanne's head slumped over onto Lyn's shoulder, and she closed her eyes. "Oh, no! What are we going to do?"

Jules turned back and yelled at Diana who was sitting in front with the driver, Tony, apparently the name of most Italian cabdrivers. "Something's wrong with Suzanne! Tell him to pull over and call 9-1-1 or else get us to a hospital quick!"

Diana's eyes were round as the moon over Rome which, by the way, had just come in view. It's a wonder the soft blue irises didn't circle in her eyeballs considering the impossible predicament she now found herself in. Natural concern over Suzanne competed violently with the quandary of how on earth to explain all this to the broken-English speaking driver. Suddenly, however, she began to think more positively. Perhaps chubby little Tony understood English better than he spoke it. It didn't look very probable, but who knew? His big dark eyes zipped about from one woman to the other, obviously wondering what was going on inside his cab.

"Tony," began Diana in her usual confident and regal manner, "one of our friends is showing signs of being in physical distress, and she needs to get to a hospital. Can you get us there or should we call 9-1-1? Is there such a thing as 9-1-1 in Italy?"

Tony's eyes grew ever larger, darting here and there and anywhere but on the road ahead. The traffic was becoming dense and almost frenzied, exactly like my travel books described. Pete and I once drove into Italy from Germany and it was like leaving a courtroom for a circus. Lyn was terrified. The headlines in the county paper changed from "Seven American Women Kidnapped by Terrorists" to "Traffic Accident in Rome Kills Seven American Women."

Magnificent old buildings shone brightly up ahead. The goal was in sight, but like the lady in my GPS box back home, we had some recalculating to do. Tony was obviously confused. At some point in the river of lovely Italian words he spewed out, Diana realized he thought she was talking about September 11, 2001 . . . a la 9/11. Consequently, Tony, who looked just like Tony in my favorite movie, *Lady and the Tramp,* was as frightened as the seven women. The cab was stalled in bumper-to-bumper traffic with the possibility that one of his passenger's middle sections was wrapped in explosives just waiting to be detonated.

Tony did the only sensible thing he could do under the circumstances. He jumped out. Flailing his arms about and screaming something indecipherable in Italian, the man went from vehicle to vehicle, warning people like Paul Revere on the eighteenth of April in 1775. Diana, lips pressed tightly together, turned to stare at Annie and me, her eyes almost as big as Tony's when he alighted from the cab. My mouth was probably as round as Diana's eyes.

"Hmm," was all that came out of you know who.

Suddenly, the three of us remembered Suzanne in the far back seat.

"How is she?" asked Annie. She could always be counted on to come forward in an emergency.

"Not good," replied Jules. "She finally mumbled that she's very weak and feels weird. But let's keep on towards the hospital. Tony can probably get us there quicker than calling an ambulance." Jules turned around.

"Where *is* Tony?"

Annie, Diana and I all looked at one another, wondering how best to answer that query. Lyn, who had seen Tony run from the cab like a chicken with his head chopped off, closed her eyes and began to pray.

Diana drew in a deep breath and finally responded to Jules. "It seems Tony has left us."

"What?!" echoed all around the vehicle and back again.

"Why?" asked Christmas in her normal pleasant voice.

"Why, what?" Annie's forehead drew low over her eyes.

"Why did Tony leave us?"

Annie stared at her, pondering the inquiry. She looked at Diana. So did Christmas and I as well as Jules. Lyn was still praying, and Suzanne was still slumped over, leaning on Lyn.

"Well," said Diana, "at this point, the question is, what do we do now, and how do we get Suzanne to the hospital?"

Jules spoke up from the back. "I don't like the looks of this."

We didn't have to wait long. Sirens began to blare like banshees on the loose. It looked as if the entire population of Rome jumped choreographically from their vehicles and ran helter-skelter down the hill towards whatever safe refuge they could find on the spur of the moment. Screaming, yelling, shouting at one another over the din of the sirens, it took only a few seconds for most everyone in sight to disappear. Lyn said she wondered if the long-awaited rapture had finally come. I don't believe in pre-trib rapture so that was one issue I didn't have to worry about. Of course, if the Lord had come, I would have gladly gone.

Until the ambulances, the fire trucks, the police, and the Italian army arrived, the only persons on that hill were seven American women in a very big taxicab—six in shock and one with a thus-far undiagnosed ailment of unknown origin.

Thankfully, Italy being a land where most public authorities speak English to some degree of expertise, we could understand the guy with the loudspeaker at his mouth. Very clearly, he said, "GET OUT OF THE VEHICLE SLOWLY, HANDS AWAY FROM YOUR SIDES!"

"Oh, dear Lord, we're being arrested! I can't believe I let y'all talk me into this trip!" Lyn was too stunned to cry.

"It's okay, darlin'," said Jules. "I'm sure these nice gentlemen will take us to the hospital. Don't you think so, Christmas?"

"Sure."

I patted Lyn on the shoulder and gave her a quick hug. "Jules is right. Just think, we may not have gotten Suzanne to the hospital in time if this hadn't happened. I'm sure it's a Divine appointment. You prayed for those, remember?"

Lyn nodded slowly. She couldn't speak.

Diana was beginning to look a bit wilted, so Annie quickly rose to the occasion. "Okay, girls, those in the outside seats, open your doors slowly and get out. Hold your arms out like they do on TV. Marnie, you talk to him when we get out."

"*Moi?*" I was in shock.

"Yes, I'm sure you'll think up something to say. You always do." Annie wasn't joking.

When we were all out of the car except Suzanne—at least a legion of the Italian army aiming guns at us—I shouted the only thing I could think of.

"*Ciao!*" That means hello or goodbye in Italian.

The man with the megaphone looked rather perplexed. He put it back to his mouth. "TELL THE OTHER PASSENGER TO GET OUT NOW!"

I began to step forward. The man was at least thirty yards away.

"STOP! DO NOT COME ANY CLOSER!" He seemed rather insistent.

Aware that my voice was not particularly strong, I circled my mouth with both hands and yelled, "Our friend is sick! She can't get out!"

Annie whispered. "They may think she has a bomb."

"Why would they think Suzanne has a bomb?" asked Christmas.

"I guess they never know who to suspect these days," replied Annie empathetically.

Lights blinked everywhere. Red, green, blue—it seemed every vehicle in sight was covered in twinkling lights. It almost felt like daytime. Actually, the sun was beginning to rise and had we not been in such a tight predicament, I would have enjoyed watching the sun rise over one of the greatest cities of all time.

Lyn was getting a headache on top of everything else. She had been crying since she arrived in the land of the Holy Roman Empire, and crying always gave her a headache. Being a suspected terrorist didn't help matters.

It soon became obvious that the man with the loudspeaker wasn't going to take my word for Suzanne's weak physical condition. "GET THAT WOMAN OUT OF THE VEHICLE NOW!"

Jules and Christmas did their best to pull Suzanne from the cab as easily and gently as possible. Thank goodness she is the lightweight in our group. Suzanne probably doesn't weigh more than one-hundred pounds soaking wet. Wobbly as a baby trying to walk, or perhaps a drunk, Suzanne managed to stand between Jules and Christmas with their full support. Her head kept flopping from side-to-side like that redheaded rag doll with the dreadlocks.

"Where are we?" she asked weakly.

"We're on the way to the hospital," replied Jules with a smile. "Don't worry. Everything is going to be all right."

"DON'T MOVE! THE DOGS ARE COMING IN!"

"Oh, Lord, not the dogs!" Lyn looked as if she might faint.

"I think I saw a CNN camera over there," said Christmas. "And there's that Fox News guy. Look! Is that Geraldo? I've always wanted to meet Geraldo!"

"Oh, I might faint! Pops will see the news! I've got to call him!" Lyn was desperate.

"Not now," I said. "They might think you're taking a weapon out of your bag."

"Oh God, oh God, please take me now . . . and Pops, too, please."

Soldiers holding Uzis in one hand and antsy German shepherds in the other, gained on their prey. After a terrifying few moments of being sniffed and poked and then scanned with some new type of borrowed Israeli technology, the leader of the canine patrol turned to the guy in charge of the whole debacle and waved an all clear sign. And that's when the army, the police, the firefighters and every journalist in Rome pounced upon seven

American women on a long awaited fun vacation in Italy.

By the time the news aired on Pops's TV in the good ol' USA, Lyn had assured him she was okay and had put me on the phone to explain. But I'm getting ahead. That was after we convinced the authorities that Suzanne was really sick and needed to get to a hospital. Of course, we were all encouraged by the very fact that Suzanne was still somewhat conscious after such a distressful ascent up one of the Seven Hills.

The man in charge—he looked a little like an Italian Ben Stein and reacted like him as well—listened to the incredible story from Annie who had been appointed speaker by the others. She sounded more believable than I and never gave more information than what was needed. Diana and I filled in details when necessary while Christmas nodded in agreement. Lyn prayed. Jules went with Suzanne into the ER cubicle.

After the guy who reminded me of Ben Stein finally put away his pad and pen with absolutely no indication of whether he believed our story or not, he slowly rose to his feet. Expressionless, he said, "Ciao, ladies. Please enjoy your holiday in Rome." And then, he and his entire entourage of soldiers and investigators and firefighters exited the hospital in quite an orderly fashion.

I was starving, and I said so.

"Me, too." Christmas grinned.

"Oh, I couldn't eat a thing," moaned Lyn.

Well aware of Lyn's aversion to any food she didn't recognize, I warned, "Now Lyn, you're going to have to eat something on this trip. Pops will never let you go anywhere again if you go home looking like death warmed over."

"I know, but I just can't stomach anything right now."

At that very moment, Jules came whirling out of the off-limits area where she had been with Suzanne for the past hour or so. "Suzanne is dehydrated. They are giving her fluid now, and she's feeling much better. Maybe a little woozy, that's all."

With a rather noisy corporate sigh of relief, we five waiting women— looking a little worse for wear—began to relax and breathe easily for the first time since we left home.

"Thank God," said Lyn, closing her eyes in prayer.

Smiling at one another with the identical prayer in our eyes, we quite erratically got up to hug Jules and each other, evidently creating a rather unusual spectacle in the waiting room where nearly everyone was Italian and had no idea what the silly American women were so happy about. However, we discovered quickly that Italians are very emotional and most of the sick souls waiting for ER service smiled happily at us amidst their suffering. One elderly lady even shuffled over to us and hugged Jules, saying *"Sono così felice per voi."* My "Italian for Travelers" pamphlet said that means, "I am so happy for you."

Laughing, Jules said, "Suzanne says for you all to go out for something to eat. I said I would stay with her and you could bring me something on the way back, but she insisted I go with you."

"Sounds like a good idea." All eyes were on Annie who always said it's important to get three balanced meals a day. No one could have discerned which meal we would be eating, but we all agreed it was a good idea.

I walked over to the desk and asked the lady in charge, "Do you have a cafeteria?"

The woman sounded as if she were saying something like cafeteria with a question mark at the end.

I recalculated. "Restaurant? Café?"

The woman just stared. Most everyone in the waiting room joined her.

Suddenly, my southern accent clicked with her. "Ah, sì! Café!" The woman's joy spread quickly. Personnel and patients alike were happy to know what the Americans wanted and just as happy to direct us to a pizza stand just outside the hospital. Everyone talked at once, giving directions in three or four different languages—possibly Italian, French, Spanish and German. The tourist season must bring the hospitals in Rome a lot of business.

"Did you get the directions?" Annie asked Diana on the way out.

"Didn't you?" Diana smiled teasingly.

"Sure, I did." Annie didn't smile. Like Lyn, she took getting lost quite seriously.

I piped in. "We'll find it. Their arms were all waving in this direction. More than likely, the stand is right around this corner."

And it was ... round that corner and quite a few more. By the time the group arrived, we wondered if it was even the same pizza stand we had been directed to. Maybe ... maybe not.

Greatly relieved by Suzanne's prognosis, we found a small table out in the sunshine and settled down to enjoy our meal. Everyone except Lyn, that is.

"What is this made of?" She stared at her plate.

"Looks like cheese, olives and tomatoes. Maybe some chick peas." Jules happily took a bite of hers.

"Chicken peas?" Lyn suddenly paled.

"No, darlin'," mumbled Jules, chewing her food.

Christmas spoke up. "Think of it like ground-up navy beans with a few spices added."

"What kind of spices?" Lyn stared at Christmas.

"Oh, Lyn, you might as well eat it," I said. "In Italy a pizza takes the place of hot dogs, hamburgers, French fries, corn dogs and any other fast food you can think of. As I said earlier, you'll starve if you don't eat *something* strange."

Diana spoke up. "Well, it isn't as if there is absolutely nothing else to eat. For dinner, we might have a nice pasta meal at the hotel or even rack of lamb. I love Italian food."

Lyn's eyes filled with tears. "I am NOT eating a sweet little lamb and neither are any of you. I just couldn't stand it."

"Here, here!" said Jules, the animal rights advocate of the group and a deeply committed vegetarian.

Diana and I locked eyes. We both adored roast lamb with mint ... or a kabob or a chop or a stew. Diana's eyes said, "Let it go," and so we did.

"Well, I guess we had better start back." Annie gathered paper plates and napkins, looking around to find the trash disposal.

"Oh, my goodness!" Lyn looked at her watch over the plate of untouched food. "We'll be late getting back."

"Fancy that," said Christmas with that twinkle in her eye.

Jules giggled. "Yeah, Suzanne certainly won't be surprised."

We disposed of the trash and then cleaned the table just as we would have at home. And then, as if in a Broadway show, we all froze in a straight chorus line.

It took a few moments to put it into words, but finally, Lyn spoke aloud what we each were thinking. "How do we get back?"

"Hmm," said Annie.

Diana sucked in her breath and held it, something she did when she didn't know what else to do. I tried to picture the map I had studied, but I couldn't seem to pull it up. Even Christmas looked a little daunted. Jules turned around and around—gracefully, of course—while Lyn started to cry again.

It was then that I spotted a red beret bobbing in and out of the growing lunch crowd. "It's him!"

The chorus line turned in perfect timing to see who *him* was. No one knew about him but Lyn, and she wasn't going to get hooked into that craziness again.

"It's that man Marnie thinks is a famous artist," she sniffled. Turning me around, she continued, "The Englishman in the restroom said you had the wrong man, remember? It can't be him so just forget it and let's get back to Suzanne. Oh, no! Suzanne is lost!"

"No," said Annie, very somberly. "Suzanne's not lost. *We* are."

"What man in the restroom?" Christmas inquired.

"Yes, what man? Was there a man in the women's restroom?" Jules's curiosity got the best of her.

Lyn glanced at me through her tears, waiting to hear how I would answer that question.

"Ah . . . well, not exactly, but that's neither here nor there. The issue is whether the man in the red beret is really Lucien d' Corsa. I think he is."

Then, at that point, lost on our first day in a foreign country, most friends would have said, "Who cares?" We seven, however, are very careful not to hurt one another's feelings and are also seriously committed to one another's ideas, outlandish as the idea might be and mine many times were . . . outlandish, that is. Consequently, we all pondered the issue for a moment before I cut into their thoughts.

"It's gone now."

"What?" Christmas looked around. Taller than the rest of us, she had a better view of the people going in and out of the small plaza.

"The red beret. That's how I found him in the airport in the first place. He always wears a red beret. I saw it on the internet." Disappointed, I turned back towards the group. They all studied my expression for a moment, and I'm sure they subconsciously came to the same conclusion my friends had come to many times before: If either of them asked another question, my answer would take much longer than time allowed.

At that moment, a strange voice asked, *"Scusi?"*

Lyn screamed.

"I am so sorry. I did not mean to frighten you, *signoras.*" The man with the voice like the Il Divo guys in harmony looked a bit like them as well. He was the proverbial tall, dark and handsome Italian with flashing eyes and talking hands. Whether he was Italian, Greek or a Spaniard, we didn't really care. He was a fine part of the scenery . . . a work of art. His eyes rested on Jules.

He spoke in a marvelous accent. "You look as though you might need help."

Jules flashed him a glowing smile. "Actually, we might at that. Our friend is in the hospital, and we don't know how to get there."

"I see. The way can be very confusing if you have not been there before." His smile outdid hers.

"Well, we . . . ." Before she could finish her sentence explaining that we had come from the hospital only an hour ago, Jules caught Diana's eye. Her head was moving only slightly back and forth from left to right, signaling that it might be better if she kept quiet about our earlier whereabouts. Diana thinks it unseemly to broadcast the fact that one has made a fool of oneself.

"No need to explain," said the good-looking stranger, still gazing at Jules. "I will be glad to escort you to the hospital."

"Oh, no need for that, just give us directions," she responded, almost blushing under his impenetrable gaze.

"No, no." Waving his tanned arms in the air, the man exclaimed, "You must allow me to escort you to the hospital! It is the least I can do for such lovely ladies in distress."

Having been a very independent single mom for nearly twenty years,

Jules's stubborn streak kicked in quickly at his insistence. "I'm sure we can find it if you will just point the way."

Diana interjected, "Jules, why don't we let *signor* . . . ." She turned to the guy, her clear blue eyes waiting for him to introduce himself.

"I apologize. My name is Mario Daniele, and I am a travel agent and part-time tour guide here in Rome." With that, he bowed at the waist as if greeting royalty, impressing us all immensely.

Diana, keeping the royalty ambiance going, gracefully extended her bejeweled and perfectly manicured hand. "Diana," was all she said.

"Diana," Mario responded. He smiled down at her like Rhett Butler when he and Scarlett weren't fighting. I nearly swooned.

The response was pretty much the same as the introductions went from one to the other around the circle our group had made in the plaza. Finally, Mario said, "Now that we are introduced, I am your friend as well as a tour guide. May I escort you to the hospital?"

Even though the invitation was obviously extended to our entire group of six, his eyes paused on Jules as if waiting for her response alone.

Caught off-guard and slightly flushed, she couldn't think of anything to say but, "That would be nice."

With keen inner sight, Diana studied the scene intently. "Mario," she said, wrapping her arm through his, "tell us about yourself as we walk. Do you enjoy your work?"

As Diana and Mario started off down the brick-laid street, our group naturally divided up into twos, rather like Noah's animals headed to the ark. Jules dallied, deliberately this time, and ended up as the caboose leaving me all alone which was fine with me.

Diana's intervention was a welcome reprieve. It had been quite a while since Jules had allowed herself to even think about men. Not because she had barred men from her life, but because there wasn't room in her daily agenda for that type of relationship. Bringing up four children alone, teaching chemistry and dance classes, along with raising horses, goats and various other species of animals filled her days to overflowing. A health nut in diet and exercise, a three-mile run had to be fitted into her daily routine as well.

Following along in her unhurried graceful pace, wearing hiking boots under a long colorful broom skirt, Jules had time to analyze her feelings for the first time in forever. Her first day in another country in years, and there she was faced with this. She was surprised at herself. Her usual smile was nowhere to be seen. She explained to me after our journey was over that even the thought of a man invading our pleasant female solidarity offended her deeply.

All this and more was trickling through her mind when, all of a sudden it seemed, the hospital came into view. A few of us were out of breath, including me, but Jules, due to her daily run and younger age, ran ahead shouting back, "I'm going to find Suzanne! Meet you in the waiting room!"

Diana glanced at Mario out of the corner of her eye. He followed Jules's every move from the moment she passed our small group until the hospital door shut behind her. Then he smiled, and although the smile was aimed at her friend, Diana nearly melted right then and there.

When she finally turned to speak to the other girls, my eyebrows were raised, indicating a million questions and ideas that were running through my somewhat overactive mind. Diana nodded in agreement to whatever they were. We often had extraordinary ideas at the same time. We both looked at Annie. She was in tune as always, but very wary according to her nature. Christmas watched it all without a word, just a gleam. Lyn was oblivious. The guy could still be a terrorist for all she knew.

A few moments later, after saying *thank you* over and over again to Mario as well as a cheerful ciao, we were thrilled to see Suzanne upright and smiling as she came through the ER doors with Jules at her side. She looked a little weak, but after assuring us she felt fine, Suzanne bubbled, quietly, with all sorts of fantastic stories about serendipitous events that had happened in the emergency room.

"You won't believe this," she began. "When I first opened my eyes after they rolled me into the cubicle, I was staring into the smiling face of a cousin of mine from North Carolina! Can you believe that?"

We easily believed it because Suzanne had cousins all over creation, and she quoted them quite often.

Everyone laughed, hugging tiny Suzanne more than she needed hugging.

"Oh, no!" Jules looked stunned. "We forgot to call B___h! He has no idea his wife has been in the hospital for the past few hours."

"I called him," replied Suzanne. "He's okay. I talked him out of flying over to take me home. Due to fact that this is football season, it didn't take long." Smiling sweetly, she added, "Let's go."

Diana took charge. "All right, girls, here's the plan. We'll call a cab to take us to the hotel. We'll rest the remainder of the day and have a nice dinner tonight. I hear the restaurant is very nice and the ambiance is unsurpassed. Sound good?"

Everyone agreed, nodding heads with a few *yeses* here and there.

"Christmas, why don't you see if you can find a taxi?"

"Sure," she said. She walked over to the desk. Within seconds, she was back, and within a few minutes, we were en route to the grand hotel close by the most famous fountain in the world, all members of our group conscious and intact.

Chapter Three

SEVEN EXHAUSTED WOMEN had never been so happy to walk inside a hotel lobby. It looked like a palace, or at the least like an extremely rich Italian's villa. We were in awe.

Love of beauty is an integral part of Diana's character. Mine, too, actually. Ordinarily, she would have ambled through the spaciously elegant lobby admiring the fine works of art and exquisite Persian carpets, tapestries and antiques. That evening, however, she was too tired to see hardly anything other than the reception counter which looked to be about a mile ahead. Thankfully, it was only a few yards.

Within those few yards, Jules began to giggle. No one turned to look at her, not even Suzanne who had thankfully gained most of her strength back. It was just Jules. She'd get over it.

But before long a giggle was bubbling up in Christmas, and she became curious to know what her insides thought were so funny. "Jules? Are we laughing about anything in particular?"

"I was just thinking about those TV shows I've heard about . . . but never watched, of course. Instead of that group of women on *Sex and the City*, we probably look more like *Desperate Housewives!*"

Christmas laughed merrily like a little girl. She was the tallest of the group but seemed more like a little child to us all. I often said it was her heart.

"Or perhaps *Mob Wives*," Christmas joked with a big grin.

Laughing rather loudly by then, Jules stopped to rearrange her bags. She was loaded down with a backpack and a shoulder bag while trying to pull her carry-on. Lyn had made a pre-trip suggestion that each woman keep her carry-on with her at all times. That way, if the luggage got lost, each of us would have clean underwear and a change of clothing if nothing else. Lyn's mother had told her never to go anywhere without a change of underwear. Mine had, too, but nowadays I counted on a Wal-Mart or Target being close by.

Suzanne, while pulling her carry-on from the curb to the counter and struggling to keep her big floppy bag on her shoulder, had recently decided to disregard Lyn's suggestion. She was still feeling a bit woozy anyway. Next flight, she would just stuff some underwear in the floppy bag and hope for the best. Just after Suzanne made that burden-lifting decision, her brain tuned in on the conversation between Jules and Christmas, and she began to laugh with them—softly, of course.

"Okay, girls," Diana interjected. "Let's pull ourselves together and rise to the occasion. This is a high-end hotel, you know."

"O . . . kay." Jules hiccupped. "We'll be good, won't we, Christmas?"

"Sure, we will." Chris winked.

"Oh, look!" I exclaimed.

"Oh, no, not that red beret again!" Lyn pulled me towards the counter.

"No, it's not that. Look at this wall of plaques. Omar Sharif stayed here! And all sorts of famous people. Look! Dean Martin and Frank Sinatra!"

"Hmm," replied Annie with a deep sigh that spoke volumes. She meant, *That might be interesting tomorrow but not now.*

Diana walked up to the counter first. She had made the reservations stateside. "Wait here, girls, in case I need you."

So there we were—seven lovely, well-dressed women looking, again, a little worse for wear, six of us huddled behind the obviously weary but always competent, regal blonde with blue eyes. The clerk glanced quickly at the confirmation printout she handed him.

With all the self-assurance in the world and a heavy Italian accent, he said, "I am so sorry, *signora,* but this is incorrect. You reserved one room for tonight with two double beds to sleep three, not three rooms."

Obviously, Diana was stunned as well as the six mute travelers behind her. "Well, I'm sorry, too, but it is definitely correct. I reserved three rooms with two adults in two of the rooms and three in the third room."

Each frazzled head behind her nodded affirmatively.

"I will see if we have two more rooms available if you would like, signora."

"I would like that because I reserved three rooms and you have the confirmation in your hand." Diana was too tired to mess around.

The clerk stared at the computer screen and scrolled and scrolled and scrolled. Finally, he looked at Diana for the first time and said, "I am sorry, signora, but there are no more rooms. We have many tourists in Rome this time of year."

"But I reserved three rooms!" Diana was growing taller by the minute, and her chest had become the most prominent part of her anatomy. "I'd like to speak to the manager, please."

"I am the manager, signora. I am sorry there was a mistake in the computer, but we have no more rooms. Would you like to keep the one room?"

Diana had traveled the world enough to know that she was headed down a dead-end road. Might as well save her dignity and acquiesce. At any rate, our stay was only for one night. We would just have to make it work somehow. Tomorrow, the group would move on to a smaller boutique hotel near the Scalinata della Trinità dei Monti, or the Spanish Steps as they're called in English, and settle in for our four-night stay in Rome.

And so, with all her weary ducklings in a fairly straight row, Diana followed the bellhop until he said, "Take this elevator, please. I will meet you in your room."

Strangely enough, the guy was waiting at the door when we all arrived. Always curious about how things work, I would have asked how he did it, but I was too tired to care. The bellhop, with a gallant swoop of his arm, opened the door and held it for all seven guests. Within no time at all, he had unloaded the cart, and Suzanne had handed him a tip from the corporate purse we had pooled for such necessities as gratuities and taxi fares. Then, we looked about the room.

It was lovely. The floors looked like white marble—whether they were or not, no one was quite sure. The stucco walls were painted a soft neutral cocoa color, and the bedding looked as if it had been borrowed from Marie Antoinette's last visit to Rome before she lost her head. Antique reproduction furniture filled the large room—two double beds, a dresser and two cane-back wing chairs with cushions in a heavy red and gold fabric.

I moved slowly about the room studying the beautifully framed art-work placed perfectly on each wall. Suddenly, I stopped. "Lyn, come here!"

Lyn was already pulling her night gown out of her carry-on. She glanced up at the surprised expression on my face and quickly walked over to me.

I was staring at the picture. "Look!"

Lyn tilted her head back to see the art through her bifocals. Squinting her eyes, she asked, "What about it?"

I tried to restrain my voice to a soft whisper this time. "It's a Lucien d' Corsa print!"

"Oh," said Lyn, narrowing her eyes to make out the signature. "Hmm, it sure is."

"I wonder if it's a sign that I'm going to meet that man in spite of every-thing."

"I don't know, but please don't go looking for him. If it's a sign, he'll show up. If it isn't, he won't. Keep it simple, Marnie."

"You always say that." I stared at the print a few more minutes after Lyn grabbed her nightgown and headed to the bathroom. She was always first to undress and first to get dressed.

Suzanne lay down on the first bed she got to. Her day had been quite exhausting, to say the least.

"Okay," Jules was saying, "Lyn and Christmas, you take one bed. Annie and Diana, the other one. Marnie always wants a rollaway because she doesn't sleep well. I'll call down and ask for a few of those big fluffy down comforters for Suzanne and me to make pallets. We'll all be snuggled up in a jiffy."

And we were.

Uncharacteristically—particularly when we seven are all together—each weary traveler was asleep in no time at all. I've always said that jet lag is sometimes a welcome aid to insomnia. Unfortunately, about an hour later, Lyn was standing over me tapping my shoulder.

"Marnie," she whispered. "Wake up. You're gritting your teeth."

"She sure is," said Diana.

Suzanne popped up. "I wondered what in the world that awful noise was."

Jules slept on, but Annie and Christmas were wide awake. I quickly joined the assembly after Lyn poked my shoulder once more.

"Oh, I'm so sorry, y'all. I should have warned you to bring earplugs. My mother said I gritted my teeth as a child. I don't know what to do about it because I never hear myself."

"I thought the correct term was to *grind* one's teeth," mumbled Diana with a yawn.

Christmas replied in her so-sweet voice, "It's according to where one is from. One from the North would say Marnie *grinds* her teeth. One from the South would say Marnie *grits* her teeth. Get it?" Christmas started giggling. "The South? Grits? Get it?"

"We get it," said Annie. Something about her tone said, "End of conversation."

"But what if I grit my teeth again." I was really worried. "You girls won't get any sleep."

"Lyn can poke you again," said Diana.

"Why don't we switch places so Lyn won't have to get out of bed to poke you?" asked Christmas.

"But you're too long for this cot. My feet reach the end, and I'm five-foot-two compared to your five-foot-nine."

"Don't worry about me. That cot is great compared to beds I've had to sleep in. The Japanese are small, you know," said Christmas, referring to her experience as a missionary in Japan.

"Okay, I'll switch with you. But turn on the light so we won't step on Suzanne and Jules."

The light blinded everyone but Jules who was still sleeping soundly and Diana who was wearing her fancy eye mask. Thankfully, neither Christmas nor I stepped on anyone, and before long we were all drifting into dreamland once again.

"Marnie?" whispered Lyn.

"Uh, huh?"

"Turn on your side."

"I thought that was to help with snoring."

"It is, but maybe it will keep you from gritting your teeth . . . or grinding . . . whatever it is."

Evidently, my tension had been gritted or grinded away because I slept silently the remainder of the night. My last thoughts were, *I wonder if that really was Lucien d' Corsa?*

⌒

Breakfast at the luxury hotel was absolutely delightful. The hotel's main restaurant extended out onto a long piazza partially enclosed by Roman columns and white stone railings. Flowering vines wove in and out and up and down, creating a scene that would catch any artist's eye. More than likely, it had been transferred to canvas time and time again.

We had finished the bountiful and relaxing Italian breakfast and were enjoying an extra cup of coffee or tea before heading out for the city center. Our first day had been set aside for settling in at the new hotel near the Trevi Fountain.

Diana said she hadn't felt so relaxed and peaceful in years—actually, since the last time she visited Italy. Like Jules, Diana was definitely not a lady of leisure and neither were we other five. Her real estate work never seemed to fit into the nine-to-five category.

This morning was different. Diana told me later that she felt as if she were in a movie. Purple and pink bougainvillea climbed the stone walls and hung from trellises overhead. Soft music played in the background, caressing Diana's tired body and weary soul. The conversation around the table was gently floating in one ear and out the other until she heard me say, ". . . Like floating down the Nile on a barge. Do you ever think about that?"

All eyes—blue, green, hazel and brown—were now on me, each waiting for an explanation. Christmas was the first to realize my question required a reply. "No, I don't recall ever thinking about floating down the Nile on a barge . . . . But I will. I'll think about it."

Jules laughed and said, "I won't. It sounds depressing."

Suzanne turned to me. "Why would you think of such a thing?"

"Oh, I didn't think it up myself. It was a scene in a book I read a while back." I always try to give credit where credit is due.

"Uh, oh," said Jules, "another book report."

"Well, do you want to know why Diana was floating down the Nile on a barge or not? I'll try not to bore . . . ."

Diana—our Diana—jumped in then with eyes wide open. "Diana? *Moi?*"

"Oh, no!" I grinned. "This Diana lived in Egypt around 1800 BC."

"Definitely not me," said Diana with a sigh of relief.

"Well, to make a very long story short," I continued, "after living a very depressing life controlled by one misogynist after the other, this Diana died. In the fashion of the Egyptians of that day, she was placed on a barge—her funeral bier—and sent floating down the Nile. I assume the ritual was symbolic of passing into another life. This was done for everyone unless one happened to be a part of Pharaoh's household. Then you got a pyramid."

Christmas interjected, "But if Pharaoh died and one lived in Pharaoh's house, one was forced to die as well, sending hundreds to their tombs way before their time. I think I'd take the barge."

"Me, too!" agreed Jules.

Suzanne was a retired high school teacher and smart as a whip. "We may have left something out here. I thought they set the barge on fire."

"Hmm, I think that's true, but I don't recall them burning Diana," I mused.

Our Diana cringed. Her face paled.

Christmas said, "My guess is that designated fire starters were stationed at the mouth of the Nile. These guys set the barges on fire before they entered the Mediterranean. Anyone who was standing around when a body was first placed on a barge upstream might have had a problem setting a human on fire, but by the time dead Diana floated down the Nile a few days, she stunk to high heaven, and the fire starters were happy to do their job." Christmas smiled.

"Yuck," croaked Lyn. "Can't we change the subject?" Her problem with foreign food was enough to deal with without our discussing decaying flesh during breakfast.

"I agree," said Diana. She looked a little green around the gills herself. "This is neither the time nor place to be discussing dead bodies, particularly one named Diana."

Annie just shook her head. The last rather smashed strawberry she was planning to eat suddenly didn't look very appetizing.

"Come on, girls." Suzanne, greatly energized by a night's sleep, urged them on. "Rome awaits!"

About an hour later, we had checked into a lovely little boutique hotel near the Spanish Steps. Diana had said it was the best place in all of Rome for our group to lodge. I had confirmed this through my many hours on the internet while Pete was watching a basketball game, a football game, a baseball game, a golf game, a race or a news talk show. I had plenty of time to surf the net.

The spacious paved courtyard seemed to be a gathering spot for travelers from all over the world. Diana and I had agreed that the charming hotel would be the perfect place for each of us to expand our cultural knowledge and refinement. People casually strolled in and out at any time of the day or night. It was my guess that Divine appointments took place there all the time, and if there was anything each of us wanted while in Rome—which some say is the second holiest city in the world—it was a Divine appointment. Doesn't everyone?

Fortunately, Diana had no problem at the registration desk. Three rooms awaited us pilgrims in the oldest section of the guesthouse, the one with stone walls and floors and lovely arches everywhere. We easily found our rooms, placed the clothing to be worn the next few days in the dresser drawers and positioned our toiletries in the spots we each claimed as our own.

I stood at the wide open window in the upper room I would share with Lyn for the next few days. A soft breeze billowed the white curtains about my shoulders, bringing back memories of previous journeys to old Jerusalem. I was amazed at the similarity. In the plaza below, people of all colors and languages milled about, laughing and talking, some eating lunch served from the guesthouse dining room. Palm trees swayed in the breeze, keeping time to the silent song my heart sang.

Being a habitual people watcher in all circumstances, but most especially in foreign countries, my gaze traveled from person to person. A tall gangly guy with dark hair and glasses leaned on a trellis post, chatting quietly with a much shorter and older dark-skinned woman. I guessed him to be Jewish of Eastern European descent. The woman was more than likely Hispanic. It was a game I had played since my first trip abroad, probably the outcome of my interest in the ancient migration of people groups to the four corners of the earth.

Leaving the window I walked out onto the small balcony to continue my game. Lyn was taking a nap, finally feeling the fatigue from the combination of jet lag and the stress of our most unusual journey. Suzanne ambled over from the room she was sharing with Jules and sat down in the only other chair on the small balcony.

I looked at her and smiled. Suzanne has been a good friend to me in the years that I have known her well. Her servant's heart is not worn, as some say, on the edge of her sleeve, but deep inside where it pours out in all manner of daily living wherever she happens to be. Like her husband, Butch, she's a very practical sort—possibly the only trait the couple hold in common—a characteristic oddly united with a deep spirituality. That unusual combination of left brain/right brain thinking is what I like about Suzanne the most, I guess. That and our shared love for writing . . . and reading . . . and painting . . . and all sorts of other things.

"Are you okay?" I asked.

"Oh, yes, I'm fine. Just a little tired from all the chaotic activity." Suzanne crossed her eyes, a comical thing she did when things were going haywire.

I laughed. "I can certainly understand that. I'm exhausted, and I didn't end up in a hospital my first day in Rome."

We laughed together, the contented familiar laughter of good friends. Silent for a while, we enjoyed the panorama before us as well as the comfortable companionship. After a bit, I told Suzanne about my game, and she readily joined in. That night I would write in my journal, *Fun is two women over fifty playing a silly game in a foreign country.*

In the midst of the peaceful courtyard scene, a hand was waving our way. It was Jules. We should have known she'd be the first to browse and mingle among the pilgrims in the plaza below. Our friend was perfectly at home. No one ever seemed strange or foreign to her. I told Suzanne it was more than likely because Jules grew up in New York City. Everyone is foreign there. She was waving both arms now, motioning for us to come down and join her.

I looked in on Lyn, and she was still sleeping—which was rather odd but greatly needed, I was sure—so I quickly wrote a note and left it on the back of the door where she would be certain to see it when she woke up. By the time Suzanne and I walked down through the palms and ferns and lush foliage, Diana and Annie were sitting at a table with Jules drinking cappuccinos.

I borrowed a chair from a baby boomer's table, delighted that they were speaking German, a language in which I could speak a few words in an emergency.

Suzanne asked the question on the tip of my tongue. "Where is Christmas?"

"Oh, she couldn't wait. She's probably at the top of the steps by now." Jules smiled. "I told her that some of us would meet her there in a little while."

"I can't believe I'm here," said Suzanne. "I guess I should pinch myself."

Jules laughed. "I understand. I always feel that way when I travel to new places. It's unreal, isn't it?"

Diana spoke up. "Rome is forever."

No one said anything as we all pondered the truth of her words. Suzanne nodded silently.

I had taken one sip of my latte when Jules jumped up and said, "I can't wait. I'm going to find Christmas at the steps." By the time she had said that much, she was sprinting as fast as her long skirt would allow. "See you soon!" her voice carried back to us.

Diana, Annie, Suzanne and I stared after Jules for only a moment when Suzanne said, mimicking an unhappy child, "I want to go."

"Me, too!" I slid out of the chair and stuffed my camera into my fanny pack which I wore as a tummy pack.

Diana and Annie were up in no time, and the four of us trudged off through the courtyard and stone alleyways to the Spanish Steps.

We had joined Jules and Christmas and were now passing out of a narrow cobblestone corridor onto the wide plaza. Italian police stood at attention here and there. One soldier, who looked a bit like Tony Bennett, was patiently listening to what sounded like complaints from an upper class Indian lady.

Noting her blue, yellow and red sari of an extremely intricate design, Jules exclaimed, "Oh, I love her outfit! Let's ask where she got that awesome fabric."

Jules took one step toward the colorfully dressed and beautifully accessorized woman when Annie pulled her back. The only thing close enough to grab was Jules's flowing hair.

"Ouch!"

"I have a strong feeling we shouldn't interrupt this conversation," whispered Annie. "Furthermore, we can't speak Indian or Pakistani or whatever."

"It's Farsi." Jules said.

I interjected with a tone of awe in my voice. "I didn't know you'd been to Iran."

"I haven't," replied Jules. "What made you think I've been to Iran?"

"Because you recognized Farsi . . . I think." More than likely, I looked as confused as Annie and Suzanne.

"Well, I have a friend who speaks Farsi, and Jules is absolutely right." Christmas had that glint of mischief in her eyes.

"Right about what?" questioned Suzanne. "I'm lost."

"So are we all," said Diana dryly.

"Come on, girls," urged Suzanne. "Those policemen are sure to think we're planning a conspiracy or something worse. We could end up in jail after all. Let's go see the Pope! I heard a nurse in the hospital say that he is in residence now."

"You can understand Italian?" Christmas was amazed.

"I could say *yes,* but I cannot tell a lie," replied Suzanne. "There's just something about a sentence with the word *Pope* in it that makes it recognizable."

"Oh." Christmas started skipping a bit, singing, "We're off to see the Pope, the wonderful Pope of Rome."

Diana, usually ready for any adventure, turned to Suzanne. "We're not really going to see the Pope, are we? I hadn't counted on that. I'm not prepared. I might faint." She looked as if her prediction might be fulfilled imminently.

"I don't think so," replied Suzanne, still a bit confused about the Farsi thing. "I doubt we could get an audience with the Pope. We're not even Catholic."

"Oh, good," replied Diana as she let out a deep breath.

I looked about the far-reaching plaza. "It doesn't look like the Pope is here, Suzanne. Actually, it seems to be a very small crowd for St. Peter's Square. I often visit those live video sites on the web. The Vatican, the Western Wall Plaza in Jerusalem, the Eiffel Tower at night—you can't imagine the places I've been."

"Oh, good," said Jules. "We'll get to dance and sing and do whatever we want to do!"

"I just want to see," said Annie, gazing at the gates to the most unique country in the world. I'll have to admit I stared at Annie for a moment, as did Diana, and considered how far Annie had come in her life. Way back when she was the dean of women at a fundamentalist Baptist college, I doubt seriously that she ever dreamed of visiting a Catholic church, must less the Vatican. It just wasn't on her agenda.

I sort of wanted to see the Pope, but I kept my thoughts to myself and followed the group over the wide plaza towards St. Peter's Basilica and the Sistine Chapel. Pete had great love and admiration for Pope John Paul II, but we hadn't come to know the new guy as yet, so I didn't force the issue.

About three or four yards from the entrance, I suddenly gasped aloud and clamped my hand over my mouth. Each of my companions turned quickly to see what the problem was. Except Jules. She was watching a wedding taking place in a smaller courtyard off the plaza.

I spun around as ladylike as possible and found five puzzled faces looking my way. Then I quickly glanced back to see how far we were from the cathedral. Noting we had a few yards to go, I whispered, "Did you see the red beret?"

Five frowning faces stared back at me as if to say, "Huh?" Lyn was still the only one who really knew what I was referring to, and she was still napping as far as I knew.

"He's about five people from the back of the line in the wedding procession," I muttered. "I'm sure he's the same man."

"What man? What are you talking about?" Jules had just clued in to our conversation.

"Whoever he is, let's discuss it later," whispered Diana.

"Okay, but don't let that red beret out of your sight." I was standing on tiptoe now, convinced that the wearer of the red beret was either Lucien d' Corsa or the man in the restroom who looked just like him. The last thought I had before reaching the awe-inspiring chapel was, *This cannot be coincidence.* After that, we entered another world.

Now, the absolutely incredible beauty of the Sistine Chapel is overwhelming. Had the Atlas bone that holds my head to my neck not given me so much pain because I couldn't take my eyes off the ceiling, the experience would have been written in my journal as one of the most enjoyable and inspiring days of my life. After all, Michelangelo himself had painted the beginning and the end up there, and I was determined to see it all and find out if he knew anything I didn't. Just to see the hand of God is an experience in and of itself, even if it isn't really His. And that thought led to another one of greater importance.

The second commandment in God's list of ten is this: "Thou shalt not make unto thee any graven image." For over fifty years I have pondered that commandment and have always come away perplexed as to the specific Divine definition of a graven image. Does it include painting pictures with whatever medium one chooses? Does it include Silly Putty animals and a child's handprints in the cement driveway? What about a crèche at Christmas?

These thoughts were still flittering through my mind when we silently exited the chapel and made our way behind the guide into St. Peter's Basilica where I discovered the highlight of my day. Again, Michelangelo was the artist at only twenty-three years of age. From a slab of marble, he sculpted *La Pieta, The Pity.* Mary is holding her son in her arms just after he was taken down from the cross. I stared at her face noting how young she was at the time she was forced to bear a sorrow too great for the oldest and wisest to carry. The guide said that Michelangelo's critics had said he had made her too young, but I, a mere admirer, adamantly disagreed. The Bible says that Mary was young, and the history of the day supports that fact.

For me, Jesus wasn't there at all. His spirit had left its earthly body, and just as it is when we lose someone we love more than life, the grieving one is left with only memories and pain, gazing at what once was. The others moved on to other sections of the huge church, but I stayed there with Mary. *Perhaps I might give her a little comfort, even now.*

When we left the Basilica, we were too overcome to talk about anything. I glanced at my friends and knew in my heart that just as I was so greatly affected by *La Pieta,* each of them held something special in their own hearts as well. Quietly, Annie suggested that we walk back to the hotel and rest a couple of hours before meeting for dinner at seven. She added that it wasn't wise to chat about anything and everything after meeting a Divine appointment. The best thing would be to rest and let the experience sink in before discussing it, even among ourselves. We all agreed, nodding affirmatively.

The fairly short walk back to the hotel was abnormally quiet. Hardly anyone said a word, and even then we spoke only when necessary. The small bookstore by the entrance to the hotel courtyard beckoned me as bookstores always do, but that day it wasn't as strong as the tug that pulled me to a little hidden garden where I sat on a bench for over an hour pondering the significance of what I had seen, what it means to the world . . . and to me.

Chapter Four

IT WOULD TAKE TOO LONG TO EXPLAIN how we came to know one another in the first place, but suffice it to say that over a period of years, seven females—now ages fifty to sixty-five and originally hailing from four different U.S. states—became the closest of friends. The diverse offshoots of seven personalities, abilities and life experiences have created a flow of endless colors which merge together to create a delightful rainbow that always seems to be on the move. Perhaps that's why we're never bored with one another. There is always something new popping up to grab our interest.

Take for instance the obvious interest Mario had shown Jules, which only Diana and I saw and Jules didn't seem to recognize at all. Of course his gorgeous dark eyes rested fairly often on Diana as well. During a scrumptious candlelight dinner of spaghetti for Lyn and various new pasta dishes for the rest of us, the two of us—Diana and I—covertly texted our thoughts on the subject while the others chatted about the events of the day and the loveliness of our hotel; very interesting subjects, indeed, but not as interesting as a romance.

Suzanne was listening to the server describe the dessert menu when a familiar smiling face appeared. "Ciao, signoras. How nice to see you again."

All eyes stared at Mario's beaming face. Suzanne, who had only heard about Mario Daniele in bits and pieces from me, was the first to get her bearings. "Hi," she replied.

"Ah, and you must be the friend who was in the hospital yesterday."

Suzanne nodded, smiling demurely.

"I hope you are feeling much better." Mario's friendly smile flashed first at Suzanne and then around the table, leaving each of us feeling as if we had been counted more special than all the rest. Swooning went out with *Gone with the Wind,* but for a moment, I wondered if we might reinstate the fad.

"Ciao, Mario," said Christmas. "Pull up a chair and sit down. We were just about to order coffee and dessert."

"I do not want to interrupt your dinner. I only wanted to greet you and see that your friend was well." Mario liked Christmas instantly. I could tell. But who didn't like Christmas?

While this exchange was going on between Christmas and Mario, Jules, who was sitting close to Suzanne, was struggling to decipher what Suzanne was saying to her out of the corner of her twisted mouth.

"What?" whispered Jules.

Suzanne managed to get out, "Nobody told me he was drop-dead gorgeous."

"He is? I hadn't noticed." Jules turned toward the guy still chatting with Christmas. "Darn . . . he sure is."

The server was patiently waiting for our dessert order. Diana pulled her gaze from Mario's face and said, "Could you bring another chair for our friend, please?"

The server nodded. "Si, signora."

In no time at all, dessert was ordered all around, and Mario's hesitation disappeared. Soon, the conversation turned lively, spirited here and there about the table by the excitement of tomorrow's more detailed trip to the Spanish Steps and Trevi Fountain. Mario, whom we all seemed to have forgotten, sat back and listened, sipping his coffee slowly. I doubt he had ever found himself in such an unusual situation—one man in the company of seven women who seemed to pay him no mind whatsoever. I learned much later, though, that he took the opportunity to study each of us without being noticed.

Jules was obviously the youngest of the group and closer to his age. Also apparent to him was the fact that the other six assumed he was interested—or should be interested—in her. He was certainly drawn to her. Then, as he watched Jules smiling and chatting away, Mario wondered if she was always so cheerful. *Probably so,* he thought, smiling to himself. She certainly seemed to be the most laid back and optimistic lady in the crowd. Yet the others piqued his interest as well. Like most Latin men, he appreciated women in general, not just as a romantic pursuit.

Although he hadn't met her earlier, Mario easily labeled Suzanne as the cute one. Witty and wise, her humor caused him to laugh over and over again. But . . . hadn't he heard someone mention a husband back in the States? Yes, he recalled, and the guy's name was Butch. *Better not to go there.*

Mario's gaze fell on Lyn, and he wondered why she only picked at her food in one of the best restaurants in Rome. Come to think of it, she looked a bit frightened . . . like a snake was on her plate.

I recognized the same expression. "Lyn, I thought you would eat dessert if nothing else!"

My poor friend looked at me as if she might cry. "I just can't eat . . . anything."

Diana said, "That's okay, Lyn. You'll feel a bit better every day, and by the end of the journey, you'll love the food as much as we do. It just takes getting used to."

Mario could see the tenderness in Diana's eyes as she smiled at her friend. She was obviously concerned, and that concern seemed to comfort Lyn a great deal. He liked that. It was the same characteristic he had admired in Diana the day before when Suzanne was in the hospital. He pictured the lovely blonde lady carrying around a protective umbrella to place over her friends when needed.

"Mario?" Annie was looking directly at him. He hoped she wasn't as sensitive to other people's thoughts as she seemed to be. "Tell us about yourself."

Startled from his long reverie, he replied, "Ahh . . . what would you like to know?"

"Well, for starters, tell us where you're from." Annie seemed to see into his soul.

Mario frowned, fidgeting somewhat. "Where I am from? I am not sure what that means."

Annie chuckled. "It's Southern for *where were you born and where do you live now?*"

"Ah, si!" His frown spread into an ear-to-ear grin, capturing the attention of every woman around the table and a few others as well. "I was born in the Veneto, in Venezia."

Jules exclaimed, "We're going to Venice in a few days!"

"You will love the Veneto. It is very unique compared with other regions of Italy."

Out of the corner of his eye, he saw Diana slightly nodding with a faint smile on her face.

He turned to her. "You have been to Venice?"

"Yes," she replied softly. "And I love it, too."

"I can see that." The two locked eyes for a moment, sending a corporate sigh around the table.

Finally, Mario asked, looking directly into Diana's eyes, "Do you have a guide for your journey to the Veneto?

"Do we?"

"Yes, you do." Mario broke his gaze from hers and turned to glance questioningly around the table. "If everyone agrees."

Six heads of a variety of clandestine colors nodded affirmatively and then turned at the same time to stare at Diana who was still looking at Mario with just the hint of a smile on her lips.

"Darn," whispered Jules to Suzanne.

"I must go now, my friends." Mario stood as he bid us goodbye. "Shall I give you my cell number?"

He seemed to be speaking to all of us, but his eyes lit on Diana and rested there while he reached in his pocket for a business card.

"Yes, thank you. We plan to drive up on Thursday and spend at least the weekend in Venice." She wrenched her gaze from Mario's dark eyes and scanned us for our responses which were, of course, very eager nods to the affirmative. Even Jules had discarded her suspicions.

"Why do I not meet you for dinner on the Grand Canal Thursday evening? We can make plans then."

"That sounds perfect," replied Diana, smiling. I thought I detected a bit of mischievousness in her smile.

Mario glanced about the table, his eyes dancing as he embraced each of us in his broad smile. "Be careful on the drive north, my friends. Stay on the main roads, and you should be perfectly safe."

"Are you concerned that women can't take care of themselves?" Jules's independent streak rose to the forefront again.

"Certainly not, signora Jules. I am sure you ladies are well able to take care of yourselves." Mario tipped his head slightly and bid us goodnight. Fourteen eyes of various colors and shades followed him across the room and up the stairs to the landing. From there, Mario looked back across the crowded room. His smile warmed us all, but it was definitely aimed at Diana who smiled back at him with a bit of a twinkle in her blue eyes.

"Wow, this is a new side of you we're seeing," said Suzanne, teasingly.

"Yeah, I didn't know you were a flirt." Jules giggled.

We all stared at Diana for a few seconds until her right ear turned so red it looked like Rudolph's nose on Christmas Eve. It was a bodily reaction Diana experienced quite often to anything deeply profound. Our friend, avoiding our inquisitive stares, turned to grab her purse and said, "I think we need to get some rest, girls. Tomorrow will be a long day."

With raised brows, we glanced back and forth from one to the other. All except Lyn. She looked at Diana and sighed. I knew what she was thinking: *Something else to pray about.*

The following day rose bright and clear, just perfect for the short walk to the Trevi Fountain.

Diana, who seemed to have forgotten last night's chemistry between her and Mario, did a quick head count. "I don't see Jules and Suzanne so that means we have time for more coffee . . . a lot of coffee." She smirked.

But, to her surprise and that of us all, Suzanne and Jules came waltzing up from the direction of the gate.

"Surprise, surprise!" Jules wore her perpetual smile.

Suzanne grinned much bigger than usual. "We couldn't wait for you lazy gals. You can see all of Rome from the top of the Steps! And Jules and I browsed through the cutest market. What's it called, Jules?"

"The *mercato.*"

"Yes, the *mercato.* It was amazing. I wanted to shop, but we knew you were waiting for us, and we didn't want to be late." Suzanne did her cross-eyed thing.

We all laughed.

"Come on, girls," said Christmas. "I can't wait to toss my three coins in the fountain."

I spent the brief walk trying to make up my mind what to wish for with my coins and wondering if quarters might work better than pennies. However, while we were oohing and ahhing over the beautiful fountain in the midst of the broad plaza, Diana turned her back to the fountain and tossed a coin over her shoulder.

"Oh! That's the way you do it," I exclaimed. "What did you wish for, Diana? Mario?"

While everyone giggled, Diana looked straight at me and replied, "You don't wish for anything, Marnie. The legend is that you will come back to Rome one day."

"Oh, great!" I turned my back and tossed my quarter, listening for the little *plink* it made as it hit the water. While the others tossed their coins, along with at least twenty more tourists, I wondered what happens to all those coins at the end of the day. Upkeep, I guessed.

Apparently, a lot of honeymooners surrounded the fountain, considering their actions. Of course, in this day and time, who knows? They may have been pre-honeymooners or just honeys. For a few moments, my thoughts turned to my husband, and I wished he could have been with me at such a lovely, romantic place. The fact that Pete and I were in our sixties, gray and bald-headed—not me, of course—didn't hinder my romantic thoughts a bit.

"Come on, Marnie." Lyn looked dejected. "Jules said we have to climb those steps over there."

When I turned around to see the legendary Spanish Steps, my jaw literally dropped. I looked at Lyn, and she looked at me. Very slowly, we each moved our heads to the left and to the right, in perfect agreement that there was no way our sixtyish bodies could make it to the top of those steps. The romantic fountain didn't make me feel old, but the Spanish Steps certainly did!

As Lyn and I stood firm in our tracks and stared, Jules and Suzanne skipped happily up the first of the steps with Christmas close behind, followed more slowly by Diana and Annie. Annie turned to us looking none too hopeful herself.

"What's up there?" I certainly didn't want to miss anything.

"A lovely French church," replied Diana, "but it's the view that everyone loves."

You will never believe it, but right at that moment, I spied Lucian d'Corsa and his red beret about ten steps up from the plaza. I caught my breath and gasped. "Lyn! It's him again!"

She looked at me as if I had lost my mind. Very deliberately, her mouth moved. "I am NOT climbing that mountain to chase that man, and you can't make me! Don't look at me like that. I'm not doing it."

"What if I have a heart attack on my way up?" I tried to look as pitiful as possible.

"I'm sure they have paramedics stationed along the way."

I hadn't seen Lyn so confident since we left home. I stared at the red beret with my hand on my heart, wondering if I could make it when I heard Lyn's voice again.

"But if I were you . . . ."

"Yes?" She looked as if there might be a better plan.

"If I were you, I would wait right over there at one of those pretty tables with me until Mr. What's His Name comes back down. He will come back down, won't he?"

"Hmm, I guess so. Good idea. Let's get something cold to drink."

Diana turned to us with questioning eyes. I motioned with my hand for them to go on without us. To tell the truth, she looked as if she thought our idea was much better.

Lucian d'Corsa did not come back down the Spanish Steps. Why? I don't know. Our friends did, though, and I spent quite a few minutes questioning them about the man in the red beret. No one saw him, not one. However, it was at that point in our journey when my friends decided they had heard enough about the man in the red beret.

Annie asked quietly, as if concerned I would be embarrassed by the question, "Don't you think you're amplifying this issue, Marnie?"

Annie said it so I at least had to consider her words. "Maybe," I replied, rather sheepishly. "But don't you think it's odd that he shows up almost everywhere we go?" I didn't wait for them to reply. "My brother always talks about synchronicity. I think it's a Freudian concept. It goes further than coincidence, and I'm beginning to think this is a perfect illustration."

"What are you talking about?" Suzanne raised her eyebrows and grinned at me.

"Yeah," said Jules, "certainly there is more than one red beret in all of Italy." She giggled and the others did also, trying not to make me feel totally ridiculous, but it was too late.

"Okay, okay. Forget Lucian d'Corsa. I'm making a resolution to forget about him and have a good time, synchronicity or not."

"That's good," said Diana, still hassling a bit from the journey up and down the Steps. "What's next?"

Christmas glanced at her itinerary. "The Coliseum."

My heart dropped. More steps, lots more.

Lyn, with face askew, spoke up. "Girls, I'm really not the least bit interested in seeing the place where all those brave Christians were eaten by lions and burned at the stake. I'm afraid it would just tear me up. I think I'll browse around the little shops near the hotel and meet you for lunch."

I quickly chimed, "Me, too. When I see the Coliseum, I want Il Divo to be there. I'll keep Lyn company."

My old friend's eyes expressed her thanks. Her confidence was growing, but getting lost was still her utmost fear.

An hour later, Lyn and I were beginning to drag. Tired and hungry, we decided to follow our little plastic pocket map to the restaurant Diana had chosen and wait there for the others. And that's where I spied the red beret once again. Embarrassed now, I really hated to mention it to Lyn, but the guy sat two tables behind her in the little sidewalk café. I had hit pay dirt. Once or twice, I opened my mouth to tell Lyn he was there, but she looked so pleasant and happy, no sign of the stress she had endured almost hourly since we left home. I couldn't bear to upset her again. But there he was, right in my hands, just like the Allstate commercial. What was I to do?

"Yoo-hoo!" Suzanne's soft voice didn't interrupt the first diner, but it did get our attention. "Lyn, I'm so glad you didn't go with us. Our guide gave really graphic descriptions of what went on in the Coliseum. I nearly threw up myself. Whatcha eating?"

While Lyn closed her eyes and swallowed her food, I gave the others a quick summary of the interesting menu. Right in the middle of, "They also have a great Mediterranean salad with . . . ," I caught myself and looked over Lyn's head to make contact with the red beret. It was gone. After a disappointed sigh that no one seemed to notice, I continued with the menu and silently congratulated myself that I had finally wised up and kept my mouth shut for once.

Chapter Five

OUR DAY SPENT TRAVELING NORTH to Venice was certainly worth writing about, but since I'm not creating a travelogue, I'll just hit a few high points. Or low points, as it were.

It's a good thing that Annie was driving because she has the amazing ability to stay focused while I, on the other hand, am drawn in by the interesting changes in the countryside, beautiful or otherwise. Suzanne spends most of her time taking pictures of vignettes she plans to paint when she gets back home. Animals seem to be her favorite subjects. I have signed copies of various foreign bovine and more Swiss chickens than you could shake a stick at. Christmas navigated for Annie while Diana admired the surroundings with me, Lyn prayed and Jules joined in on everything.

We were moving right along on one of those wide European autobahns when—all of a sudden, it seemed—we were on a narrow four-lane, and the traffic began to slow to what might be called a creep. I hadn't really noticed until we found ourselves in the left lane of bumper-to-bumper traffic and I was sitting on the right side of the vehicle with no view except the cars beside us.

I pushed myself up to the back of the front seat. "What's happening?"

Diana did the same, eager to find out why we were suddenly stopped on what we thought was the major freeway between Rome and Venice. Jules crawled over the back seat and joined the huddle. I was so impressed by her agility that I almost got off track with what was going on.

Suzanne said, "These cars are blocking my panoramic view."

Well, let me tell you, Annie always has a serious expression on her face, but this time that same expression had drooped into a frown. Even

Christmas looked a bit daunted, glancing up and down from the map in her lap to the road ahead.

"Well?" said Diana. "Do we know what is going on?"

"No, we don't," replied Annie with not a hint of a smile on her face.

Christmas didn't actually look worried, just a little confused. Before we could think of anything else to ask, she rolled down her window and stuck her head outside, quickly grabbing the attention of the good-looking, dark-skinned soldier in the vehicle beside us.

"Ciao!"

I couldn't help but smile, wondering how many times Christmas had said her one Italian word over the past two days. "Do you speak English?" As I've said before, Christmas is a very friendly person and everyone likes her, even right off.

"Do I speak English?!" The guy grinned big time. "Why, I'm from Georgia, ma'am. Where're you from?"

The grin on her face expanded like someone had turned up the dimmer on a light switch. "I'm from Texas," she replied, laughing. "And my friends are from North Carolina except for one, and she's a transplanted Yankee! We love her, though."

"What are you gals doin' on this road?"

We were moving so slowly by then that it was as if the guy from Georgia and Christmas were sitting side-by-side in the living room.

"We're going to Venice!" replied Christmas, shouting over the noise of the traffic and a few helicopters overhead.

"Venice? Ma'am, you're not going to Venice, not today."

"We're not?" Diana had, by this time, stuck her head out our back window to join the conversation. She liked meeting new people as much as Christmas, especially Southerners.

I glanced at Annie. She was doing what I admired her most for, focusing on the road. Suzanne had put away her camera to get in on the conversation, too. Lyn was waking up, and apparently, by the worried look on her face, just getting the drift of what was going on.

"Where *are* we going, Georgia?" Jules crammed her slender body between me, Diana and the door.

"Are you the transplanted Yankee?" Georgia had the whitest teeth I've ever seen.

"Yep, that's me," replied Jules with a big smile.

"Well, ma'am, you sound like a Carolina girl to me!"

"I've been in the South a long time, Georgia. I got there as quick as I could after I was born."

We all laughed at that, except Annie. She sighed so deeply we heard it above all the noise.

Christmas waved her arm out in the direction we were headed. "Can we exit up ahead? We're supposed to meet someone in Venice at seven p.m."

"No, ma'am. You are now on American soil. You are entering Caserma Ederle, home of the 107 Airborne, United States Army!"

In perfect unison, we all yelled, "What?!!!!"

"Yes, ma'am! And you can't turn around or pass go or collect two hundred dollars. I guess you don't have a pass, huh?" Georgia threw his head back and laughed from his gut.

"A pass?" Christmas said. We all stared at Georgia with mouths hanging wide open.

"I was just kidding, Texas." He laughed again. "When you get to the guard post, a soldier will come to your window and ask what you're doing here."

"What *are* we doing here?" Christmas glanced back at Annie who just shrugged her shoulders and sighed. She hadn't cracked a smile yet.

Diana spoke up. "Will they believe that we're just lost?"

"Well, normally, I would say *yes,* but since we took out Osama bin Laden just five months ago, you might encounter a few problems. The entire base is on high alert, you know."

Lyn closed her eyes and leaned her head on the side of the car, covering her face with both hands as tears poured down her cheeks. "Oh, God," she prayed, "deliver us from this mess and get me home. I promise you and Pops I'll never leave again."

Georgia continued his instructions, looking around at Annie the best he could. "Just roll your window down, ma'am, and wait for them. Don't say anything; just answer their questions."

"Will they speak English?" I knew we couldn't say ciao to everything.

"Oh, sure, they're Americans, remember?" Georgia flashed his white teeth again. "Just be calm. I doubt they'll think that seven white women with Southern accents are terrorists." Laughing hysterically at his joke, Georgia noticed the car ahead of him was speeding up. "Gotta go, gals! Y'all have fun!"

"Bye, Georgia! And thank you!" We all shouted as Annie pressed the gas pedal.

Within minutes, an Italian van filled with seven silent women pulled through the gates of the United States Army base somewhere near the Veneto in the nation of Italy. I wondered what Caserma Ederle meant, but I didn't dare ask. The Bible says there's a time to speak and a time to be quiet—I think—and this was definitely a time to keep my mouth shut.

"Oh, God, help us!" Those were the first words from anyone in quite a while, and they didn't come from Lyn. They came from Annie. We were stunned.

"What's wrong now, Annie?" Lyn knew that if Annie was praying out loud the picture was looking ever worse.

Looming ahead of our van, high in the air and nearly filling our view of the sky was a gigantic sign with three lines. The second line, the highlighted one, read, "DEFCON CHARLIE!" All I could think about was how happy I was that the top line, "DEFCON DELTA," was not lit up, but the other girls seemed to be beside themselves with worry. Perhaps they didn't realize that we were not in all-out war, not yet anyway.

"Oh, God, why on earth did we come to Italy in the middle of this mess?" Lyn was looking heavenward now, so I knew her mental and nervous condition was worsening.

Diana reached back and patted her knee. "Lyn, we didn't know that, after ten years, our boys would get bin Laden just a few months before our vacation."

"Well, we should have thought about it." I was surprised at Lyn's miffed tone of voice. She is usually very kind.

Annie rolled her window down, watching a young soldier with a gun slung on his shoulder walk very deliberately towards our van.

Bending a little to see inside, he looked first at Annie who was staring straight ahead and then at each of us as if we were in a criminal lineup. However, I will have to say that his face showed no judgment as to whether we were guilty of anything or not. Christmas still thinks he was trying not to laugh, but I didn't notice any humor whatsoever. Anyway, why would he laugh? We were perfectly normal American women except for Lyn who was quietly weeping and praying in the far back seat.

"Where are you ladies headed?" He spoke with no sign of emotion, sort of like that Ben Stein guy back in Rome.

"Venice," Annie almost whispered.

I think I did detect a bit of humor at that point. The sergeant's closed mouth twitched a little.

"Start the vehicle, ma'am. Your escort will arrive shortly."

I guessed he was Southern, too, but I hated to ask. Another time to be silent.

Without another word, the sergeant walked away. And that's when we heard the siren that got closer and closer until a vehicle with a blinking light on top drove straight towards us and then did the quickest three-point turn I've ever seen. The driver threw his arm out the window and waved for Annie to follow. To this day, neither I, nor any of my friends, have any idea how we got on that army base or how we got off other than that we followed the vehicle with the blinking light and siren for quite a few miles until he suddenly exited the highway and signaled for us to drive on.

"Want me to drive?" asked Diana. Annie shot back a look that blocked any other ideas Diana might have had.

As I leaned my head back on my travel pillow and closed my eyes, I heard Jules whisper to Suzanne, "Why didn't we take the train?"

Chapter Six

I CAN'T REMEMBER EXACTLY WHEN Christmas came into our lives, but I do remember that she became friends with Annie first. I'll have to check with Annie, but I think the two of them met when they were both involved in the same fundamentalist denomination, where Annie had been the dean of women. She was also a much sought-after speaker. Christmas, of course, was a missionary to Japan, and to this day, she and Ken Chan go back to Japan every few years.

Christmas is one of the kindest people I know. With a compassion born of her own suffering, she bonds with children of every age and brings healing to the child within without a self-help book to tell her how. A paradox in so many ways, our tall Texan friend has the sweet voice of a child and the gentle smile to go with it. Christmas also sings, writes songs and plays the guitar. That's why one of our favorite pastimes when we are together is singing. While Christmas and Diana strum away, the rest of us join in—sometimes harmoniously, sometimes not. The only Italian songs we knew were in English by Dean Martin and Frank Sinatra, and we were belting them out at the top of our lungs. That's what we were doing when Annie drove our lease van towards the bridge and we inhaled our first view of perhaps the world's most unique and fascinating city.

From that moment on, we were enthralled with Venice. The smells—from fish markets to tantalizing Venetian restaurants—were my first impressions, along with color and music and light and, of course, water everywhere. Before we could reach our hotel, situated conveniently on the Grand Canal, my right brain was taking all sorts of exciting rabbit trails this way and that, and my left brain was wondering how on earth we could see all this magnificent city had to offer in only three days. Finally, as our water taxi pulled up at our lovely hotel, I rested in the thought that Diana, the well-qualified leader of this venture, knew my favorite natural and cultural pursuits as well as her own and had planned to suit. I just hoped my eyes wouldn't boggle out and my mouth would stay somewhat closed as I took in the delights of the ancient city.

My dear friends were obviously as mesmerized as I was. I honestly believe that not one of us would have remembered to pick up our weekend bags if the elegant valets hadn't taken them inside for us. By the way, I have noticed—since flying Al Italia with the Italian Soccer team in 1994—that all Italian men are drop-dead gorgeous. I couldn't help but wonder, as I followed my own personal valet into the exquisite lobby, if there had been some sort of mutant strain in the line of Adam somewhere and all the plain men ended up in Russia, all the handsome guys in Italy and those in between were scattered all over the remainder of the known world.

Now, if there is one thing I do admire in men, it is promptness, and Mario Daniele was waiting for us by the desk in the restaurant at exactly seven o'clock. I apologize for continuing to refer to Il Divo, but remember the one with the little wayward curl dangling on his forehead? I think he's a Spaniard, but he must have those same Latin genes because Mario could have been his twin brother. He couldn't have been that happy to see seven American women—four of them older than he—but he certainly acted like he was. The hostess must have thought we were royalty, the way he greeted us.

About halfway through dinner, I realized that the more elderly among us, me included, should have declined Mario's dinner invitation and opted for room service instead. Our entire day had been not only exhausting but traumatic, if one could call getting lost and finding ourselves on a U.S. Army base in Italy—one nearly at war at that—traumatic. We certainly wouldn't have had to feign an excuse to decline a dinner invitation. But alas, common sense hadn't clicked in—not even Annie's—and we found ourselves gathered around a lovely mahogany table set beautifully with mixed spring flowers and silver accessories, eating uncommonly delicious dishes I had scarcely heard of. Most of them ended in *inni*.

There are times in my life when I get a second chance to use the common sense I have heretofore ignored. Thankfully, this was one of them.

"Mario, this evening has been wonderful, but I have to admit that I am exhausted from our long and harrowing day and so, before dessert is ordered, I must beg to be excused so that I can rest my weary bones and my somewhat overactive mind."

Before I could say *boo,* Mario was up and politely holding my chair as I pushed away from the table. Lyn looked as if she was praising the Lord for the door I had opened while Annie quickly put her napkin on the table and stood without any assistance.

"I understand, signora Marnie," crooned Mario. "Tomorrow will be a very active day as well. You must get your beauty rest."

I didn't say anything, but it wasn't my beauty I was concerned about.

Lyn and Annie were obviously too tired to bid the others goodnight, but before we had time to gather up our bags, Christmas had joined us as well as Suzanne. That left Jules and Diana at the table with Il Divo number five, and I'll have to say that they both looked very pleased.

The five of us party-poopers wound our way between the lovely tables and out into the main lobby of the hotel. Right at Suzanne's heels, I leaned forward and whispered, "Why didn't you stay? You're among the younger group, you know."

"Have you forgotten about Butch," she whispered back, chuckling and crossing her eyes at the same time.

"Actually, I did. But I guess it's pretty hard to forget about Butch if you're married to him, huh?"

"Yes, it is."

I thought I caught a glimpse of a smile.

"I think I'll give him a call and tell him about the day's adventure. He'll get a kick out of the army thing." Suzanne gave me a quick hug and unlocked her door as I followed Lyn into our room.

"Are you going to tell Pops about today?" I asked.

"Not until we get home."

"Good idea."

Chapter Seven

HAVE YOU EVER WONDERED how on earth the Italians, or whatever they were at the time, built the city of Venice in the first place? Well, I have and now I know, but it would take too long to explain, and I'm sure that story wouldn't be as interesting as the one I'm going to tell you.

We were on our way to the center of Venice and the first Jewish ghetto in the world, created, interestingly enough, in 1492. In fact, the word *ghetto* was first coined in Venice. It really means *foundry* because it replaced an ancient foundry.

Gliding along as smooth as silk through the wide canals, I sat as close to the gondolier as possible so that I could hear what he said, but nobody said much of anything due to the tranquility of the delightful journey. Colorful laundry hung high up from building to building, something I had always wanted to see but not have to do. Silently, I expressed my thanks for washers and dryers and anything else that kept my old-age underwear from being displayed to the public. I was tempted to close my eyes and enjoy the ride, but I was afraid I might miss something. The scenery was truly incredible, nothing like anything I had ever seen.

Graciously helped from the gondola by our gondolier as well as Mario Daniele, I quickly gained my land legs, adjusted my fanny pack and geared myself up for a day of walking.

"Now," said Diana, smartly dressed in a crisp sea-blue tunic and white pants, "Mario has offered to guide us through the ghetto as a favor, and I'm sure we are all very appreciative."

That was an understated understatement, and we all knew it, considering our budget. As flashing smiles and sparkling eyes flowed towards our good-looking benefactor, all seven of us silently thanked God as well.

Diana's relationship with Mario Daniele seemed to rise and fall in temperature. Not his temperature, but hers. His seemed to be getting increasingly warm, piping hot at times. However, Diana—the friend it was sometimes hard to read—seemed to be living in the tropics at one moment and in the Arctic at another. I could tell Mario didn't quite know what to make of her. Nonetheless, his interest in her did not wane. Not one bit. In fact, Diana's temperature changes were evidently luring him on.

"Well, Mario, you're in charge," said Diana, smiling blue eyes matching her tunic.

I don't know what made me think about it at that moment—perhaps because Diana turned the day over to Mario—but one thing that all seven of us have in common is an extreme unwillingness to be controlled. We've never discussed it, but each of us exhibits that characteristic clearly, even though, oddly enough, not one of us could be classified as a feminist. Nevertheless, that lovely October day in enchanting Venice, we took great delight in being controlled by the most handsome man on the street. We obeyed everything he said, decently and in order as the apostle Paul said for women to do. At least, I think that's what he said.

Cannaregio, the residential district in which lies the Jewish ghetto, is delightful, and I would have enjoyed browsing around there all day, but the sights and sounds of the first home of Jews fleeing the Spanish Inquisition called me like a clarion from above. Mario had arranged for a local Jewish rabbi to lead us through the museums, the synagogue and other places of interest. As anyone who knows me well might guess, I have another entire journal describing this trail of our journey, but I won't take time to share it with you now because, as we were exiting Cannaregio, Suzanne turned to me and said, "Marnie, look behind you about, say, five people. Do you see what I see?"

"Oh, my goodness!" The red beret shone in the bright sunlight like a beacon on a hill, except the hill was Lucien d'Corsa's head.

"Is that him?" Suzanne, the first of the sisters to actually see the red beret other than Lyn, now truly believed me. I was thrilled, to say the least, and much relieved.

"Try not to let him see you," I whispered.

"Why? He doesn't know me from Adam." Suzanne was right, of course.

"Well, don't let him see *me!* He might remember me from the men's restroom and that would be terrible."

"Hmm," said Suzanne sounding a bit like Annie. "That picture might be hard to forget."

"What's he doing now?" I stared straight ahead, hoping the others wouldn't realize we were lagging behind until I decided what to do.

"Well, to tell the truth, I think he's looking at you, or *for* you."

I stopped dead in my tracks. "What? Why would he be looking for me?"

"Because he thinks you're crazy and he wants to turn you in to the men in white coats, that's why." Suzanne smiled in that witty way of hers.

"Come on," I said, grabbing Suzanne's hand to pull her along. "Let's catch up with the others and get out of here."

"I thought you wanted to speak to him?" She changed to her hurry gear.

"Well, I did, but now I don't. He didn't like me, and now I don't like him. He's obviously not really Lucien d'Corsa because anyone who paints like that would be nice. But that theory doesn't always prove true. I saw a movie about Beethoven, and he was mean. And Cezanne was weird. And they say that Degas was . . . well, I won't even go there." Even though Suzanne was pounds lighter than me and younger, she was huffing to keep up my pace and talk at the same time.

"Glance back when you get a chance," I said.

We had already passed our group and had nearly made it to the gondola thingy. The girls might have thought we were acting strange, but they didn't notice because all eyes were on Mario who was evidently explaining something interesting about Venice which I would like to have heard if I'd had time.

"Marn, I'm pretty sure he's following you. This is really weird."

"Ciao!" I said to the gondolier. "Jump in, Suzanne!"

Surprised at the quick action of two middle-aged women, the old guy spilled out a few phrases neither of us understood and to which I replied, "Hurry! Go! *Veet, veet! Alle, alle!*"

He must have understood one of my languages because in no time, we were cruising up the canal at an unusual speed for a gondola, at least it seemed to me. After a few minutes of fast paddling, or whatever one calls it, he said something and shrugged his shoulders as his hands flew up in the air.

"What's he saying, Suzanne?"

"I think he wants to know where we're going. Where *are* we going, Marn?"

"Anywhere will do, but let's just go back to the hotel. The others can find us there."

"Sounds good. Tell him." Suzanne crossed her eyes again. One of these days, she's not going to be able to uncross them. That's what my grandmother said, anyway.

Thank goodness, I could pronounce the name of the hotel, for when I said it, our little guy grinned great big and said, "Si! Si!"

In no time, we were there, hearts still pounding and totally exhausted from another exciting but stressful day in Italy. Just as we alighted from the gondola, aided by our polite but rather confused gondolier, Suzanne said, "Look, Mar."

And there he was. Lucien d'Corsa, red beret still perched atop his not very handsome head, floated by in his own private gondola and pretended he didn't even see us.

"Do you think he was following us?" I asked Suzanne, a shiver sprinting down my spine.

"Of course, he was," she replied. "But why?"

"That's what I want to know."

⌒

That night at dinner, tucked away in a quaint little sidewalk café eating mussels and all sorts of antipasti with our Chianti, Suzanne pulled herself up to her full height and drew in her breath. "Girls," she began, and then remembered Mario, "and Mario, of course. I guess you're wondering why Marnie and I came back ahead of you this afternoon."

Everyone nodded in agreement, including Mario.

"Well, it's a long story, but the bottom line is that I saw the red beret and I saw Lucien d'Corsa or whoever he is. I can now vouch for Marnie. She has not lost her mind . . . yet."

"Oh, thank God," gasped Lyn.

"He's real, that's for sure." Suzanne looked dead serious.

Annie said, "Hmm."

Jules popped up. "So why does he show up everywhere we go? I still think there is more than one person in a red beret."

"No, no, it's him alright," replied Suzanne while Lyn nodded in agreement.

"Strange," said Diana.

"Sure is," said Christmas.

Mario hadn't said a word. He knew nothing of my embarrassing exploit in the airport restroom, and I hoped no one would deem it necessary to tell him. Thank goodness, no one did. Suzanne briefly explained that Lucien d'Corsa was an artist I admired and how strange it was that either d'Corsa or his double had appeared nearly everywhere we had been so far.

Mario very politely listened to Suzanne's synopsis, glancing at each of us from time to time.

"Marnie," his voice sounded as if he were singing my name, "I must tell you that I like d'Corsa's art, too."

"Oh, how wonderful! I was beginning to think I dreamed him up." I smiled at Mario and even reached over to touch his hand.

"He is a very well-known artist in Italy, and I would easily recognize him, I think, even in a crowd like today. And you are right. He does often wear a red beret, but he is not tall as you described this other man. D'Corsa is actually rather short and a bit stout."

"Oh, shoot," I quipped. "And all this time I thought I was going to meet the great artist."

Lyn's eyes said, *I told you so.*

"So, who is following Marnie, or all of us, around Italy?" I was glad Jules was finally into this thing.

"All I know is this means the man is up to no good," said Lyn frowning.

"You're right," said Annie, and we all turned to listen. "Perhaps we'd better get the police in on this." She looked straight at Mario.

"Perhaps, but not yet," he replied. "This man has not done anything that would interest the authorities. We are not even sure he is following anyone. It could be coincidence."

"You're right," said Diana. "He could be a tourist who just happened to visit the same places we have. Nothing strange about that."

"I just have a feeling there's more to it. Don't you, Suzanne?"

"I'm not sure. Today, I would have said *yes* when he went floating by in that gondola. But now, I don't know. Maybe he thinks it's weird that we show up everywhere *he* goes."

"Well, I can't prove it, but I can't help but believe he's following somebody," I said.

"Don't you dare try to prove it!" Lyn's reaction shocked us all. "I see those wheels turning in your brain, Marnie. I mean it! I'll get on a plane and go home if you don't leave this thing alone and let us get back to our vacation."

The others stared at me, waiting for my response. They knew I didn't have a choice.

"Okay. I promise I'll leave it alone." *Unless I see him again.*

Mario must have read my thoughts. "If you see him again—you or Suzanne or Lyn—show this man to me, and I can watch out for him as well."

"Me, too," said Christmas, followed by Jules, Diana and even Annie.

Silence filled the air for an uneasy few moments until Jules spoke. "I think I hear music down the street. Come on, maybe someone's dancing!"

And they were, right there on the edge of the Grand Canal, band and everything. Wonderful Italian music filled the air along with the chitter-chatter and laughter of people having good fun. Although Jules's dancing was usually of a different genre, she joined right in the crowd, and Mario was right behind her, obviously delighted to be her partner. We girls found a table close to the dancers and made ourselves comfortable to be the watchers, sipping our wine, making light conversation and enjoying the show.

Bless Mario's heart, he made a point to dance with each of us during that delightful evening. The weather was warm with just a tiny bit of breeze blowing in from somewhere—the Adriatic Sea, I guess, if my map memory serves me correctly. The music, the wine, the soft lapping water—

every little detail of that delicious evening added to my delight and, I'm sure, the other sisters' as well.

Diana certainly enjoyed herself. Mario graciously ushered her into dances almost forgotten in the past few years of her busy life. I loved watching them. He would waltz off with Diana for a while and then swing back to switch to Jules, never forgetting to offer each of us older sorts his hand in between. Even Lyn, who had danced rarely since her cheerleading days in high school, got a'hold of that "Woman, Thou art Loosed" idea and showed us a thing or two. Suzanne nearly fainted, having no idea Lyn had it in her.

It would be an understatement to say that Italian men are not shy, so I won't say it. Any willing female was led onto the dance floor with the utmost of gallantry, flashing smiles and dark, curly hair. That's why it wasn't long before our dancing little Jules was passed around like a ballerina gracefully spinning on top a music box. She was having the time of her life. Although extremely fulfilling, teaching little children how to worship God through dance was a bit different than cutting loose where no one knows one amid twinkling lights, handsome men and the Grand Canal of Venice. Every now and then, Jules would pop back into sight, smile and wave, and then spin off into the moonlight.

Christmas, Annie, Suzanne and I mostly watched, enjoying ourselves immensely.

"You know," said Suzanne, "Italy is good for us. Most of us are descendants of the British culture, and I think that makes us a bit uptight."

"More than a bit, I'd say." I laughed at the thought of how uptight I had been in my life.

"I wonder how the British ended up so stuffy." Suzanne was just musing as was often the case. While we pondered her query, Diana and Mario came into view, slowly dancing to a song that was not written for slow dancing. She casually tossed her blonde head back and looked into his dark eyes with a bright smile, obviously responding to some humorous remark he had made.

"Looks like Diana has overcome her British stuffiness," said Christmas with a mischievous smile.

"Sure does," said Suzanne.

"Hmmmm . . . ." said Annie.

"Oh, I wish Butch liked to dance." Suzanne sighed softly, her eyes filled with hopes for a more romantic future.

"Pete used to dance," I commented, "but I never could keep up."

Christmas said she danced in her heart and I knew exactly what she meant. I have danced in my lifetime, but never freely nor with one iota of talent or agility.

"You might not believe this," I said to the girls around the table, "but when I was a young girl, I often dreamed of dancing."

Christmas smiled, and I knew she understood.

"I dreamed of dancing like Ginger Rogers and Fred Astaire, that type of thing . . . even though they were way before my time, of course. In my dreams, I was lithe and light, and I moved as if my body and the music were one." My eyes closed and once again, I danced with the stars.

"That's what heaven will be," said Annie softly.

"Yes," said Christmas, "you'll dance like that in heaven, Marnie."

I smiled. How sweet my friends were. And how thankful I was that they understood.

Chapter Eight

THAT LAST NIGHT IN THE HEART OF VENICE—lights twinkling on the water, music and dancers and lovers all around us—seemed to settle in all of our hearts as the unsurpassed experience of our journey to date. Those of us who had husbands missed them terribly, and those who didn't missed theirs more. There couldn't have been a more romantic spot in the entire world.

From that time on, there was a noticeable change in the relationship between our Diana and Mario Daniele. As gracious as he was handsome, Mario tried his best to treat us all equally, but each of us detected his preference for our lovely blonde friend with the blue eyes.

As we settled into our rental van for our half-day's journey south to Florence, Jules wiggled in between Suzanne and me, giggling as quietly as she could.

"What's so funny?" I asked.

"Yeah, what's up?" Suzanne and I leaned around Jules so we both could hear her reply.

"Have you noticed the budding romance?" Jules continued to smile and giggle.

"We're not blind," said Suzanne with a cute smirk.

"Where were you last night, girl?" I chuckled and gave Jules a quick hug.

"She was floating on moonlight and music." Suzanne made a funny face.

"That's right," I agreed. "You probably didn't know that Diana and Mario danced for hours without even a restroom break."

"No!"

"Yes, and when we walked back to the hotel, they were still dancing. Even though the crowd was diminishing, we could tell the musicians were winding down." I stared at Jules, my eyes squinted. "Where were you, by the way?"

"I don't really know," whispered Jules. "Did you know that there are sidewalk cafés and dance floors all up and down the canal?"

"It's a wonder you didn't get lost." Suzanne crossed her eyes again.

"Lost? Who got lost?" Lyn popped up from her place beside Annie.

"Don't worry, Lyn. Nobody got lost." I leaned around Jules again and whispered, "I do hope we don't end up on that army base on the way back. Lyn will just die."

At that point, we all settled back to enjoy the lovely Italian countryside, en route to Florence, the art capital of Italy and the heart of Tuscany.

$$\frown$$

Most of my favorite light-hearted movies take place in Italy. That fact had never crossed my mind until the ride down to Florence or Firenze as they say in Italy. The six of us in the back (Diana was riding shotgun with Mario, but she joined in as well) recalled the scenery in various movies we had seen. *My House in Umbria, Tea with Mussolini, Enchanted April*—all were filled with the music, Italian accents and awesome landscapes of the Italian countryside.

"I feel as if I've been here many times," said Suzanne, my partner in movies of any kind.

"Me, too," I replied, my mouth agape at the beautiful vineyards stretching over hill and dale and disappearing into the broad horizon. Small huts and large villas were wrapped in grape vines creating a continuity of color that was extremely pleasing to the eye.

"Deja vous?" asked Christmas smiling.

"Not unless you can count movies as having been in a place," said Suzanne with a chuckle. "We have lived vicariously, I guess you'd say."

"Well, no more!" I had secret dreams of owning a villa in Italy someday—a place where Pete and I could peacefully live out our days and the seven sisters and other friends and family could come and play. I envisioned a combination of *My House in Umbria* and the villa in *Enchanted April*, only smaller. I didn't want high maintenance, but I did want a flower garden like Maggie Smith's . . . and a gardener.

Christmas leaned up between Jules's head and mine and whispered, "I gotta go potty. How do we tell Mario?"

Jules spoke up. "Mario! We have to pee!"

You could have put a roll of toilet tissue in my mouth and Suzanne's. Out of the corner of my eye, I saw Diana turn towards the side window, shunning us all. As for Mario, he was laughing hysterically along with Christmas who was just happy that Jules hadn't mentioned her name.

Lyn turned around and whispered to Jules. "I'm so glad you said something. I think I'm going to wet my pants. I just hope I don't sneeze."

Mario pulled the van over to a place that looked as if the inhabitants were peasants in medieval times. Pete and I always search out places the locals frequent when we travel, and this place was definitely one of those. I was delighted. Diana didn't look too sure. I could tell she was concerned about the cleanliness, but the ethnic charm of the place overcame any trepidation I might have had. I could tell Lyn was more worried about her overflowing bladder than anything else.

Mario decided it was a good time to fill the van with gas or petrol or whatever they call it in Italy. The little gas station, café and produce stand were what some tourists might call quaint and others would call run down. Between the van and the door, I decided on quaint. There was no sense in being negative, and what's more, we would see how a different class of people lived compared to the classy Venetians and the middle class Romans we had met so far.

The small stone building looked as if it had once been painted a lovely yellow ochre and fitted with a green awning on which was painted, "Luigi's," in faded red. Being a winter on the color chart, I lean towards bright colors which made me think that about fifty years ago, this was probably an adorable little pit stop between Venice and Florence. Rather than cute little tables and chairs on the dirt patio, old wine barrels were turned upside down and scattered about. A few customers stood at them eating like at hot dog stands in the States.

Before I got one foot inside the door, Lyn and Jules met me head-on coming out. "Did you find the restroom?"

"Luigi pointed us in this direction," said Jules.

"Outside?" I asked.

"I guess so." Jules eyes twinkled while Lyn frowned.

The three of us rounded the small building as if on a treasure hunt and quickly discovered something akin to an outhouse I visited once around 1953 in the hills of Appalachia. There were, of course, many in my area of eastern North Carolina in those days as well. Having never visited an outhouse, Jules saw it as an adventure, but Lyn groaned aloud and sighed until her chin was touching her chest. As for me, I was still trying to think *quaint*.

When Jules opened that weathered wooden door and the breezes of Tuscany wafted through the crooked boards of the outhouse to our noses, we looked at one another and made an unspoken decision to close the door and never look back. We quickly retraced our steps around the little store and entered the place at our own risk. Annie, Suzanne and Christmas were paying for bottles of cold water and perusing the odd assortment of merchandise in Luigi's store.

Annie asked, "Where is Diana?"

"She's standing by the van chatting with Mario," Jules replied with a grin. We quickly exited the tiny dim-lighted building and took no time in telling the others that the restroom was unusable, defunct, as Pete often says.

"Bad, huh?" asked Christmas.

"Worse than you can imagine," replied Lyn. "And if I don't find a restroom soon, we're going to have another problem."

The six of us moseyed out to the van discussing the possibility of another gas station in the nearby vicinity. Piling one by one into the van, we settled down for what we hoped was a short ride. Mario and Diana turned away from the ancient gas pump and headed towards the store to pay Luigi for our fuel. We must have all been watching them, thinking about the new turn of events in Diana's love life when just before they reached the door of the store where Luigi stood smiling at his good fortune, Diana turned and started toward the restroom she didn't know was a stinky old outhouse.

The reason I know we were all watching them was that each one of the six sisters in the van yelled something akin to, "No, Diana!" forgetting that old Luigi's eyes were lecherously following our lovely friend as she walked regally towards the unknown. All three of them looked back at us at the same time—Luigi, Mario and Diana—each obviously questioning our severe command.

Thank goodness, Diana understood us first. As graciously as a Southern lady could possibly be portrayed in *Gone with the Wind*, she slowly turned and asked with an element of surprise in her voice, "I don't have to go to the restroom? Oh, I thought I did."

Six heads—all stuck out one window or the other—went back and forth from side to side, indicating a definite, "No, you do NOT have to go to the restroom."

Slowly, and oh, so gracefully, Diana walked back to the van as if she were on a model's runway while Luigi wondered what was going on and Mario flashed that incredible smile once again.

Chapter Nine

NO WONDER DIANA HAD RAVED SO MUCH about Florence. And no wonder the little old British ladies in *Tea with Mussolini* had refused to leave when the Nazis invaded and took over. The city may not be quite as romantic as Venice nor as wild and exciting as Rome, but its pure beauty cannot be surpassed. Everywhere I turned stood a gorgeous fountain with one Roman god or the other as its centerpiece, usually naked as a jay bird. And then there is David, Michelangelo's masterpiece and the favorite sculpture of all womankind. The Bible says that David was a handsome man, and I must say that Michelangelo did an incredible job expressing it. However, if one stands studying the statue any length of time—especially if that one is accompanied by someone of Mario Daniele's physique and if that one is female—one's pulse begins to accelerate as one's face grows redder by the minute. Oh, it happens.

"Just think," said Suzanne, "no artist before nor since has ever equaled Michelangelo."

I was so proud of Suzanne. She seemed to be totally absorbed in art appreciation with no thought of David's nudity.

"Why don't we stroll on down and see my favorite frescoes," said Diana who was blushing worse than anyone except Lyn, that is. But she had strolled on long ago. She just could not force herself to stare at a naked man in public, she told me later.

It was at the grave of Robert and Elizabeth Browning—she being one of my favorite poets, by the way—that Diana's heart flipped to another level in her appreciation of Mario Daniele. I actually saw it happen with my own eyes as well as my intuitive sensibilities when it regards my sisters.

All eight of us were standing in a wavy semicircle, admiring the tombstone and probably trying to remember all the words to "How Do I Love Thee?" when Mario casually opened his sensuous mouth and began to speak.

"Art is much, but love is more. O Art, my Art, tho'rt much, but Love is more! Art symbolizes heaven, but Love is God and makes heaven."

Silence is good. It gives you time to get yourself together and that's exactly what each of us did in our own ways. Most of us followed that long silence with a sigh of some degree, all but Diana. She was obviously overcome and deeply touched by our gorgeous Italian's rendering of the last lines of *Aurora Leigh* by Elizabeth Barrett Browning, of course. I watched to see how she would respond, and I'm pretty sure the other five sisters joined me. We were not disappointed.

Turning her emotion-filled face up to his, our Diana spoke softly. "That was beautiful, Mario."

His smile was all that was needed in reply. In retrospect, I wish I had clocked that moment—in time or out, I do not know—in which no one moved or said a word. While Diana gazed into Mario's eyes and he into hers, we stared at them with unabashed interest. I tell you, it wasn't long before I felt like I had at the statue of David. Nevertheless, it seemed almost unholy to interrupt the moment. But, thankfully, before I could think what to do, we were saved by another small group of Browning admirers who had come to visit the grave.

Without a word, our group of eight headed back to the street and on to our next destination, each of us intent on our personal interpretation of what had happened in, oddly enough, an Italian cemetery at a British poet's graveside. Later, I reminded Diana that the number eight means new beginnings. She was delighted at the thought whether it meant anything or not.

That first day in Florence seemed almost surreal, as if I were walking around in a glorious recurring dream, and I guess I really was for I had dreamed of being there all my life. Our apartment near the Piazza della Signoria was quite lovely and efficient as well. It even boasted a couple of Botticelli reproductions as well as a few very nice antiques that Diana, our antique collector, highly admired as did we all.

By late afternoon, my heart was aching to continue our walking tour of the great art of Florence, but my body was aching to get somewhere and rest. When I expressed my need, the others agreed that perhaps we were pushing ourselves, striving to get too much done in one day. Our plan was to stay in Florence three nights, hoping to see as much as possible in that short amount of time.

The only negative about our nice apartment was that beautiful ancient buildings seldom have elevators and my aging joints simply require an elevator. But we had to make do, and having Mario around helped immensely. He seemed to know everybody in Italy, and when we needed someone to carry our luggage or shopping bags up two flights of stairs, three or four young boys showed up on the spot. It was really amazing. I never did see him ask anyone to help us. They just appeared out of nowhere, younger versions of Mario and the Italian soccer team.

I shared a room with Christmas this time, and because she never seems to need an afternoon repose, I found myself all alone, lying on an antique canopy bed with white bedding. A soft Tuscan breeze came through the open window, gently billowing the soft white curtains and cooling my weary body.

As Dorkas Lane says in *Lark Rise to Candleford* (one of my favorite BBC series), "my one weakness" is that when I lie down to rest, my mind doesn't. It stays fully alert and occupied with all sorts of topics from the day's activities to plans for tomorrow and right on into the next year. My mind will not even slide into low gear, much less park.

And so, as I was lying there on the white bed wishing I could take a nap, I got so antsy that I arose from my bed to see what was the matter. (I just couldn't help that!) I pattered across the lovely terracotta tiled floor and stood at the window a while, enjoying the gentle breeze and the sights of the piazza from above, including Neptune's nude body.

And that's when I saw him. I tell you, my heart jumped right out of my chest and my head felt dizzy enough to faint. I may have even shrieked, although not so loud as to disturb anyone in the next room. Lucien d'Corsa—or his lookalike—stood like a sentinel beside the fountain, his tall, thin frame making quite a contrast with the virulent Neptune.

This time, from my covert watchtower, I was able to study him long enough to notice two outstanding facts. Number one, he was always alone, and number two, he was obviously watching the entrance to *our* building. I decided then and there that I would not allow myself to be talked out of believing that this man, whoever he might be, was following our little group all over Italy.

He watched the door, and I watched him. And then, I had the idea to clock him, wondering if he would remain on guard until we exited the building. I assumed we sisters were all resting while Mario was out and about doing whatever he normally did. Remembering that we were having our dinner catered in that evening, I found myself chuckling aloud at the thought of signor d'Corsa standing there at the fountain all night. He was going to have a long wait.

It didn't take long for the man to outstand me. I decided to lie down again and pray my mind would settle down as well. If d'Corsa was still in his spot when I arose, I would march myself right down there and confront him. If he was gone, I would share my discovery with our group during dinner, and we could then discuss what to do about our little problem— that a man in a red beret, pretending to be a famous artist, was tailing us throughout Italy. It was unnerving, to say the least.

Just so you'll know . . . I slept for an hour.

Chapter Ten

WHEN I AROSE, our stalker was still at his post. *Oh, good,* I thought. I slipped on my bedroom shoes and hurried out the door, hoping someone was awake so that I could prove Lucien d'Corsa was following us. Thank goodness, Christmas was tuning up her guitar in the living room or *il soggiorno* as they call it in Italy which, if you ask me, is too much to say for something as simple as living room.

"Hey, Marnie. Whatcha doin'?"

"Christmas," I began, taking a seat beside her on the sofa and forgetting my plan was to confront our stalker, "you won't believe this, but the man that I thought was Lucien d'Corsa is standing at the fountain with Neptune and he's watching our building. He's been there for at least two hours."

"Really?" Christmas strapped a capo on her guitar.

"Yes. He's following us, Christmas. I just know he is."

She smiled and hummed a few notes, tuning the instrument. "But why would he be following us? He's not the Italian CIA, that's for sure. We have no information worth their time and effort." Christmas beamed a smile at me and giggled. "Can't you just imagine us being interrogated by the Italian CIA with bright lights and all that stuff?"

I sat silent for a few moments, a little bell ringing somewhere in my overactive mind.

"Christmas! That's it! You may have accidentally figured this thing out." I smiled at her, my mouth open.

"I did?" She was as amazed as I was. "What did I figure?"

"Remember when Suzanne got sick on the way into Rome and we were sort of arrested?"

"Yeah, that was exciting. I saw Geraldo, remember?"

"Yes, I do, although I'm not sure it was Geraldo." I frowned in thought a second or two.

"Sure, it was. Mustache and all."

"Well, anyway, that inspector who looked and spoke like Ben Stein, remember him?"

"Yeah."

"Well, I think he told us to stay out of trouble or something like that. I bet he didn't trust us and he put this guy on our tail. That's not a very nice way to put it, but you know what I mean."

"I guess he could have done that," said Christmas in her soft voice. "But I think it would be a waste of the government's time and money to chase seven old women around."

"That's true, but it's been my experience that governments are not concerned about wasting money, and more than likely, time is not of the essence either. By George, I think you've got it, Christmas!"

"Wow," she said, smiling all over. "I'm smarter than I thought."

Diana had heard Christmas tuning up the guitar and came into the room ready to join the sing-along. Jules followed on her heels.

Leaning closer to Christmas, I whispered, "Let's wait until after dinner to tell the others when we're all together. I guess Mario will be here as well, don't you?"

"My guess is he's going to be with us the entire trip," whispered Christmas, grinning at Diana.

Before long, we were singing the cutest little song Christmas had written about a rabbit who played in the forest. Annie, Lyn and Suzanne joined us as we transitioned into "Sugar Time" and "The Yellow Rose of Texas." I must say, we have a very broad repertoire. We were really getting into the harmony of "How Great Thou Art" when the most tantalizing aromas started wafting in from the kitchen. How the caterers got in, I don't know, but they were welcomed with open arms. I do believe that was the best meal we had during our vacation up until then, made even better because we were dressed in sloppy clothes and perfectly relaxed around our own table. Mario wasn't even there, just the sisters, and I'll have to say that it was a very special evening even though I had hoped Mario would be there when I shared the new revelation Christmas and I had just received.

And sure enough, Mario came in later after coffee and dessert—the most delicious tiramisu I've ever eaten. We heard knocking at the door, and Diana smiled like Juliet when she asked, "Wherefore art thou, Romeo?" and then spied Romeo in the crowd.

"Why don't you get the door, Annie?" Diana obviously thought it improper for her to be the first to greet our new friend and her *whatever.*

Mario entered the room flashing his gorgeous smile around for all of us to enjoy. And we certainly did. Not only did we appreciate his fascinating looks, but the Mario within had grown on us as well. He was a good person. I just knew it. I find it amazing how God networks people, even in foreign countries. My mind went back to that synchronicity thing again.

Lyn offered Mario dessert and coffee which he declined for a glass of red wine. I noticed he didn't take the first chair available but walked a few extra steps to sit on the sofa, evidently hoping Diana would sit beside him. And she did.

I could hardly wait to speak. Hours had gone by since I first spotted d'Corsa by the fountain, and except for telling Christmas, I had kept it to myself. I can't tell you how proud I was of my deportment. However, I could hold it in no longer. But before I began, I stood and walked over to the window to see if d'Corsa was still there. He was and thank goodness he didn't see me because this time he was speaking with someone, a big guy who looked a little like Marlon Brando.

"What are you doing, Marnie?" Bless her heart. Suzanne always expresses interest in my activities.

Walking back to my chair, I replied, "Well, girls—and Mario—I have something to tell you." All eyes were on me as I perched on the edge of my seat.

"Lucien d'Corsa, or whoever he is, has been watching our building all afternoon and evening, and he's still there."

All eyes lit up. "Really?" asked Jules as Lyn's jaw dropped.

"Yes, I saw him from my window when I went to rest. He's been standing by the fountain all day, and girls, I *know* now that he is definitely following us."

Mario walked to another window and looked out. "She's right. That guy with the red beret is standing by the fountain talking to another guy." Mario retook his seat by Diana, a little closer this time, I noted.

Suzanne was the one who asked the $64,000 question: "But why would anyone be following us?"

"Well, Christmas may have figured that out," I replied.

Christmas grinned as she softly said, "And I didn't even know it."

"We were thinking all this over earlier this evening while Christmas was tuning her guitar. She mentioned the CIA for some reason I can't recall, and then we remembered our little adventure being interrogated by the police in Rome."

Mario looked a bit startled. "Wait one moment, *per favore*. Why were you being interrogated by the police?"

Diana patted Mario's hand. "It's a long story and much too complicated to get into now."

"Were you arrested?" he asked, obviously interested in this new insight into our activities and, possibly, our characters as well.

"Oh, no," said Diana. "They let us go after a couple of hours."

"That's why I think Lucien d'Corsa has something to do with that rather frightening experience. What if that policeman still suspects us of being troublemakers? What if he put an APD on us and assigned the guy I thought was Lucien d'Corsa to us?"

"It's APB, Marn," said Suzanne.

"Oh, okay, whatever. Well? What do you all think?" I waited with bated breath, just knowing I was correct in my assessment of the situation.

"You may be right, signora Marnie, but I cannot imagine you ladies doing anything that would require a stakeout at your apartment." Mario slowly shook his head, disbelievingly.

Lyn was listening intently, wiping an eye with a tissue every now and then. Not surprisingly, Annie hadn't said a word. She was processing.

"Yeah, Marnie. We didn't do anything that bad," said Jules, laughing at the memory.

I could tell that set Mario's wheels spinning. He frowned and looked at Jules, clearly wondering just how serious our actions in Rome had been.

"I don't know all the answers," I replied, "but it's a fact that this guy is stalking us for some reason. Every time I've spotted him since we first arrived in Venice, I suspected it, but now, with him standing watch outside our building all day, it's a proven fact. Oh, and except for tonight, he's usually alone. Have you noticed that, Lyn?"

"No," she answered, almost in a whisper.

"Well, no matter what the reason, something is going on," stated Suzanne emphatically. "Now the question is, what do we do about it?"

Mario eased up to the edge of the sofa, his knee against Diana's. "I suggest that in the morning I make a visit to my old friend at the Firenze police station, Inspector Franco. If this has anything to do with the police in Roma, I am sure they would have notified their colleagues in Florence. What do you say?"

Mario glanced about the room receiving affirmative nods from each of us.

"But what if this has nothing to do with the police? What will we do then?" Lyn was almost on the verge of tears which concerned me greatly because she had been doing so much better since that peaceful evening on the Grand Canal.

"Let us follow this path first," replied Mario. "If it comes to a dead end, we will pursue another option."

"That's a very wise plan," said Annie.

"Why don't you make your visit to the Inspector early," suggested Diana. "Then we can get on with our day, I hope."

Mario smiled down at Diana and gave her a wink which embarrassed her to no end and apparently thrilled her as well.

When I went to bed that night, I was thankful for two extra blessings: one, that I could tell I was going to sleep well, and two, that I was allowed to be a firsthand witness to the first love affair in our little group of friends.

Chapter Eleven

DURING ONE OF MY REGULAR TRIPS to the bathroom that night, I came to the conclusion, more like presumption, that Mario would discover that, sure enough, his friend, Inspector Franco, had been alerted by the police in Rome that a group of seven "middle-aged" ladies might cause a few problems and should be watched. Contrariwise, on my last little trek around five a.m., I suddenly remembered that I first saw Lucien d'Corsa in the airport restroom in Rome, hours before our entanglement with the police on the freeway. I always find it amazing how, in one split second, everything can change. The so-called revelation Christmas and I had, Mario's idea and plan, none of them were true. And there I was at five o'clock in the morning with no one awake to tell.

Tossing and tumbling, I finally drifted back to sleep in time to be awakened by a whiff of bold Italian blend and my roommate's cheerful, *"Buon giorno,* Marnie!"

"Mornin', Christmas," I mumbled.

"Sorry to wake you up, but Lyn and Annie cooked a big Southern breakfast, and they want everyone to eat it. Didn't you sleep well?"

"Not particularly," I groaned. "But at least there's a reason." I pushed myself into a sitting position and thought fleetingly about playing hooky all day. "Is Mario here yet?"

"I think he's in the kitchen watching Diana think." The comical little giggle Christmas lets out every now and then can start me laughing at the wrong time if I'm not careful.

"Okay, I'm up," I said, planting both feet on the cool tiled floor. "Do I have time for a shower?"

"I don't think so. Annie says scrambled eggs won't stay warm without getting rubbery."

"That's true," I agreed.

Christmas and I arrived in the kitchen just as the others were taking their seats around the long farmhouse table. I loved that the apartment had a long table in the kitchen as well as the dining room. We could be formal or informal according to our mood and with seven women, we were in and out of moods like we were in and out of the bathroom.

Having been taught that upsetting topics can disrupt one's digestion, I kept my new theory to myself until most of us were on our final cups of coffee. Mario had evidently been brought up the same way, and for that I was grateful. Good manners are essential no matter what country. He didn't say a word about his visit to the police station until the last egg was swallowed.

"My friends," he began, "Inspector Franco informed me that he has heard nothing from the police in Rome regarding seven American ladies. And, he knows nothing about a man in a red beret although he is familiar with the art of Lucien d'Corsa. I am afraid that leaves us at the dead end we spoke of last night." Mario glanced around the table awaiting a response, his eyes resting on me.

"Well," I began in my usual way, which always reminds me of Ronald Reagan, "early this morning, it dawned on me that I first met this guy in the red beret in the airport restroom. If you girls allow your minds to drift back over our first few hours in Rome, you will recall that my meeting him there was probably a couple of hours before Suzanne got sick and we became involved with the Roman police."

Christmas giggled. "Roman police. Can't you just picture those guys in togas with laurel wreaths on their heads?"

Mario smiled at Christmas. "I like you very much, my new friend."

"I like you, too, Mario." She sounded like a baby chick.

My friends didn't seem to be taking my report too seriously. "Do you understand what I'm saying? There is *no* way the government could have anything to do with our constant pursuer. And that means he's up to no good, more no good than we thought."

I paused to let that sink in. It did.

"You mean he might be planning to hurt someone?" Lyn's eyes bulged somewhat.

"I hope not, but who knows? He's stalking us for a reason, and we now know that he's not one of the good guys."

"He doesn't even have a white hat." Christmas wasn't joking.

"Mario," said Suzanne, "is he outside the building today?"

"No, I did not see him this morning."

"I guess criminals have to rest sometime," said Jules.

Annie stared at the cup in her hands and murmured, "What on earth could he want with us?"

We waited for the answer that never came. Silence filled the room except for the slow tick-tock of a round black clock on the kitchen wall.

Throughout the day, I found myself looking back over my shoulder for the red beret. I think the others were watching for him as well, but no one said anything. Just after lunch, I had another revelation: *The man obviously didn't care if we knew he was following us.* I mean, would you wear a red hat if you were trying to stalk someone? I pondered that thought for the rest of the afternoon, and sadly, I honestly didn't enjoy the beauties of Florence that day. My mind was too preoccupied with the mystery that had somehow interrupted our long-awaited vacation. On top of that was concern that one of us might be hurt or kidnapped or worse.

By three p.m., Lyn gave in to her anxieties. "I just can't stand it. I'm going back to the apartment and rest. I can't get my mind on art and culture today. I think I'll write Pops a postcard."

"I'll go with you." If the truth be told, I was as fed up and as worried as Lyn although I hated to admit it, even to myself.

In the end, we all decided to go back except Diana, Jules and Mario who opted for the planned trek up to the Piazza d' Michelangelo from which you could see the entire city of Florence. I couldn't have made it halfway, but I did so mourn the loss of that incredible view later when I saw it on the internet.

As we parted, Diana spoke softly so no one but me could hear. "Lyn was progressing so well. I just hate that all this has set her back."

"I do, too, but I'm praying the mystery will be resolved quickly so she can enjoy herself again. For all our sakes. This craziness is messing up our vacation."

That afternoon, Annie had a long talk with Lyn. It's a bit strange that with Lyn's great faith, she is so prone to worry. My theory is that it's generational, and since I'm of the same generation, we're working on that issue together. Annie certainly helped.

⁓

The following day was our third and last in our lovely Florentine apartment. I could hardly bear to leave. Because of our abnormal circumstances, there hadn't been time to ride out into the beautiful Tuscan countryside. We hadn't even visited a winery or any of the Catholic shrines scattered along the highways and byways of Italy. I'm not Catholic, but I do think they are interesting and quite convenient for travelers. A little roadside altar here and there wouldn't hurt us Protestants one bit.

Just before we were to check out of the apartment, I stood out on our little balcony looking for the red beret and at the same time wishing with all my heart that we didn't have to leave Tuscany. I had fallen in love, and I couldn't bear to part from my beloved.

I heard someone's soft steps, and then Diana appeared beside me and placed both hands on the balcony rail. For a few moments, we just stood there, enjoying our view of Florence one last time together.

"Marnie?"

"Hmm?"

"I have an idea, more like a change of plans idea."

I looked into Diana's blue eyes and discovered an excited twinkle. "What's up your sleeve?"

"I cannot bear to leave Tuscany, Marn. We just haven't had our fill."

"Oh, my goodness. I was just thinking the same thing!" Diana and I often have the same grand idea at the same time, so it shouldn't have been a surprise.

"Let's don't leave. Florence, yes, but not Tuscany. Let me call our travel agent and rent a villa in the country. Or perhaps Mario knows of something we'd like." She smiled, blushing slightly.

"That's a great idea! Oh, I am so relieved. I actually thought I might cry all day like Lyn."

"What about the others? Do you think they will agree? I talked to Annie a few minutes ago, and she's up for it."

"Well, they said in the very beginning that the plans were up to us. They were happy not to have to make the decisions."

"That's true. Let's go talk to everyone before we check out."

Every single one of us agreed with Diana's plan, even Lyn who thought she might feel more at home in the country. Within minutes Diana had made a phone call and given the person on the other end our preferences. Within minutes after that, right after Mario arrived with the rental van, the agent called back and gave her the address for our Tuscan villa, my dream come true.

I believe in signs, as you may have guessed, and the sign to confirm our villa for me was confirmed in its name—Anna. My great grandmother's name was Anna as well as my daughter's and her daughter, my first grandchild. My dream of a garden like Maggie Smith's in *My House in Umbria* was fulfilled as well with a gardener to boot . . . and a cook! I cannot express my love and that of my sisters' for that amazing plot of heaven on earth. We will never forget it.

Mario had already shared with Diana that he would have to leave us a few days for a job he was committed to before we arrived. And so, as he left on the back of a friend's motorcycle, Diana waved a smiling but tearful goodbye, and we settled down to enjoy our blissful paradise.

The first day or two we walked about the property in a trance.

"It's as if we're in a movie," said Suzanne, awe in her voice.

"Yes, and we're the stars," Jules replied, happily floating along the garden pathway.

Even Lyn looked positively affected by our new surroundings. "I wonder if the rapture came and we're really in heaven. I read that the flowers in heaven are more colorful than those on earth, and these certainly seem to be." Lyn leaned down to smell a giant pink and white peony.

"It could be that the rapture came and we got left behind. Remember that book?" Mischief was written all over Christmas's face. "God may have had mercy on us because we didn't make it so He left us in this beautiful place."

"Or," Suzanne added, recalling our day at the Vatican, "we *could be* in purgatory.

"Hmm . . . ," said Annie, smiling this time. "I never thought of purgatory as being beautiful, even if there is such a place and I'm fairly sure there isn't."

"Me neither," I said, "but I guess purgatory could be beautiful. Let's ask Angelica, the cook. Everyone seems to be Catholic around here."

Always tactful and considerate, Diana asked, "Might she not be offended?"

"Oh, I don't think so," replied Christmas. "We chatted while she cooked breakfast this morning, and she has a great sense of humor. We've come to know one another pretty well. I'm sure she would be willing to explain anything we'd like to know."

Suzanne, who teaches English as a second language, quickly caught a glitch in what Christmas said. "But Angelica only speaks a few words of English."

"That's right," I replied, my curiosity piqued. "Did you have a translator, Christmas?"

"No," said Christmas, softly. "I just listened with my heart."

Knowing Christmas like we did, not a one of us questioned her simple explanation. Actually, it added an even more heaven-like feel to the Divine property we had miraculously acquired.

Augmenting the beauty as well as the amenities of our villa was a gorgeous kidney-shaped swimming pool. We discovered it on the second day. We slowly strolled down the rose-covered path and soon came in sight of the lovely blue pool surrounded by a wide patio of remarkable Italian stone, flanked with all sorts of flowering trees and greenery. The hundreds of house and garden magazines hidden all over my house in closets, drawers and the attic couldn't have possibly contained a picture to compare with the landscape before our eyes.

As we stood there in a horizontal line taking in the incredible beauty of a newly discovered area of our little heaven, I guessed that the majority of the others were thinking the same thing I was thinking. I might never stick one toe into that startlingly blue water, but who cared? Just the splendor of the place had already restored my weary soul.

We spent our days in the trance that overcame us upon our arrival. We took walks on lovely paths to we knew not where. We read whatever we wanted, whenever we wanted, hidden away on quaint garden benches in vine-covered arbors and trellises or seated on the stone piazza in deep, cushioned lounge chairs. Some days, I even stayed in bed, writing with inspiration that flowed through the open doors into my room on the translucent wings of a gentle breeze.

Jules, the only runner in our group (she's the youngest, remember?) discovered new and exquisite landscapes for us to explore every day. I had always fancied one of those romantic picnics with a red-checked cloth spread out on the ground—grapes, cheese and olive bread to eat and red wine to cap it off, complete with wine glasses and pretty cloth napkins. It's rather hard to have a romantic picnic with seven women and no men, but we made the best of it and enjoyed ourselves immensely. Mario would return in a few days and at least we would have the pleasure of watching him and Diana enjoy a romantic picnic. I dreamed of Pete and exhaled. He once prepared a little picnic for me at an overlook on the Blue Ridge Parkway, wine glasses and everything. He wouldn't sit down, though, because he didn't want to get dirty, and that sort of took away from the romance.

Oh, the cuisine of Tuscany! Is there anyone on earth who doesn't love Italian food? Not one in our seven, that's for sure, not even Lyn. We discovered that our American idea of Italian food was quite limited. Angelica filled the long antique walnut farm table with incredible delights, every morning and night after night. Lunch was on our own, but there were always plenty of leftovers in the fridge. Each area of Italy has its own specialties as does each cook, and Angelica outdid herself. By the end of our stay, we all wanted to take her home with us. Diana and Annie even started spinning ideas for an Italian restaurant in their back-to-business heads.

Can you imagine having absolutely *nothing* to do? I couldn't and neither could my special friends. In a million years, I could not describe the feeling of living through even one day with no responsibilities whatsoever other than my personal hygiene. I didn't even have to make my bed or hang my clothes in the antique walnut wardrobe. A tiny but buxom girl named Pisa—born in sight of the leaning tower and named accordingly—flittered around the large villa like Casper the Friendly Ghost, quietly gathering up anything that didn't belong and finding the appropriate place to put it.

"How does she know what belongs to whom?" Lyn and I were watching her from the balcony above the large but cozy living room.

"Evidently, Pisa already knows each of us well enough to match us up with our clutter. It must be her gift."

"She's amazing," said Lyn, shaking her head in awe.

My friend of too many years to count has worked hard all her life. Being a hair dresser and a farmer's wife, physical labor was no stranger to her, and it was a struggle for her to accept having a maid, much less a cook. It was all I could do some days to keep her from helping Pisa and Angelica. Then she wanted to pay them.

"They came with the villa," Diana explained.

"Oh, my goodness. We'll owe a fortune, Diana." Lyn's worried expression came back from wherever it was hiding.

"Don't worry, my friend," Diana assured her. "No one will have to pay one extra *lira* over our original budget."

Lyn expressed her relief with a deep breath in and a rather loud sigh. I stared at Diana in shock. I shouldn't have been surprised, being very familiar with her way with people as well as her business expertise. But this deal was akin to the miraculous and hard to believe. Diana beamed a mysterious smile at me and turned away, knowing it would take another miracle for me not to ask how she did it.

Chapter Twelve

I GUESS I SHOULD CREDIT some of the peace we felt in Italy to the fact that not one of us had experienced the urge to go shopping during the entire trip. We had browsed through markets on our way to other destinations, of course, but that deep-seated female longing to shop—particularly in a foreign country—had not yet arisen. Finally, the day before Mario was scheduled to return, we hopped on the bicycles awaiting our use and rode about a mile into a little village Angelica had suggested.

Passing vineyards ready for the harvest and olive groves with ladders leaning against the trees for the pickers, it was all I could do to keep my eyes on the road ahead and not bump into Annie who just in front of me.

"Why don't we stop and see if they will let us help pick olives," I shouted. "I think they will because I saw it in *Under the Tuscan Sun!*

"I'd love to do that, too, Marnie," yelled Jules from behind me, "but Angelica said that the markets close fairly early because they open at daybreak, and we were late getting started."

I think Diana placed Jules behind me so I wouldn't stray down a rabbit trail or stop to rest too many times. Each of us had literally gone into training, each in our own way, in anticipation of our long awaited journey. My preparation had consisted of walking Pete's treadmill while the ladies on *The View* argued and Bill O'Reilly assured his guests that they were wrong and he was right. You can get in a lot of time exercising that way, and that day, I was grateful for it.

When we rode into the little hamlet, half expecting to see the citizens wearing Etruscan clothing or at least Roman togas and those one-shoulder-strap gowns on the women, we were overcome with the sights and smells of a real Italian *mercato*. Nothing was "put on" for tourists, and I would guess that the villagers were surprised to watch our elderly convoy ride into town like a very nice bunch of Hell's Angels. Later, when I shared that thought with the others, we had a good laugh when Christmas changed the name to Heaven's Angels, a much more appropriate name for seven Christian women even if we were Protestant in a Catholic country.

We parked our bicycles in a fairly convenient place and paid a little guy who looked a bit like Pinocchio with a short nose to guard them.

"Look at this!" Jules exclaimed. "You'd think we were in a foreign country!"

That set us all laughing to beat the band. Jules had to suppress giggles the rest of the day.

Colorful tents and awnings set the tone for the excitement of market day in the little village. And under every one—most of them heralding the red, green and white of the Italian flag—were tons of fresh vegetables, fruits, freshly picked olives, pistachio nuts, tons of garlic and everything one might equate with Italian farming.

We browsed through the booths, tasting this, that and the other although there was nothing we really needed because Angelica had done her shopping hours earlier. However, as we turned a slight corner in the narrow cobblestone street, the most gorgeous Italian pottery you've ever seen caught my eye. I would have bought it all if I'd had the money and a truck to haul it back to the States in. While Suzanne, Lyn and I stood drooling over the pottery, the others sauntered on down to the antique section which I wanted to visit as well. I just couldn't pull myself away from the colorful Tuscan pottery.

As we were deciding which piece, or pieces, to buy as souvenirs of our journey to the Tuscan countryside, I suddenly felt Suzanne stiffen beside me. She grabbed the hand with which I was feeling the pottery—women have to feel the merchandise, you know—and jerked me in the direction she was staring. There he was, Lucien d'Corsa, in living color, red beret and all. He was pretending to choose which ceramic platter he wanted, but we knew he was watching us out of the corner of his eye.

"Psst," I hissed to Lyn. "Look over there by the big orange pots."

Her hand involuntarily flew to her mouth. "Oh, no," she whispered, her eyes nearly bulging out of her head.

"What should we do, Marn?" Suzanne was such a humble soul. She was willing to lead or follow, whichever was best for all.

"There's nothing we can do," I whispered, feeling the pottery again so I would look natural. It certainly wouldn't do for d'Corsa to know we'd seen him. But then I thought, *Why not? He never seemed to care before.*

"Let's just act very nonchalant and stroll on down to the antiques and warn the others that he's here." I turned away slowly, hoping I looked totally engrossed in shopping. Suzanne really was engrossed. She was determined to buy a ceramic Italian rooster no matter what our stalker did.

"Come on down after you pay the man," I said, prodding Lyn in the right direction.

"Are you just going to leave me to get kidnapped or worse?" Suzanne didn't cross her eyes this time. She was as serious as she could be.

"I'm sorry. I guess I didn't think he'd do anything in broad daylight and in a crowd of people."

"Well, you never know. Stay right here until the vendor gives me my change back. You need to help me make sure I get the correct change, too." Suzanne handed the man her cash.

"I still haven't gotten the exchange rate settled in my head," I replied. "Euros are easy but these little places that still use liras baffle me. Liras make one sound so rich."

Lyn placed a hand on both our shoulders. "I'm going to catch up with the others, okay? It makes me nervous to be near that man."

"Sure, go ahead. Just don't get lost," I teased.

"Why did you have to say that?" Lyn looked not only nervous but peeved as well.

It seemed my friends were a little testy that day, but I couldn't blame them. The mystery of the guy in the red beret was getting to all of us.

After we counted Suzanne's change and decided that if we had been robbed, it wasn't enough to make a fuss about, the two of us walked as casually as we could down the cobblestone street to the place where Diana was admiring an exquisite settee made of wood I didn't recognize.

She didn't seem surprised by my arrival even though Lyn hadn't said anything yet about our previous encounter. "Are you going to buy it?"

"I'm thinking about it." Diana, our antiques aficionada, was carrying out the female feeling thing to the nth degree.

"Where will you put it?" asked pragmatic Annie.

"On her back, probably," said Christmas, laughing.

One by one, we each joined in the joke, picturing our dignified Diana all hunched over, struggling to get through the airport with a settee on her back. For a few moments, I totally forgot we were being stalked. It's amazing what a little laughter can do.

Diana spoke up. "I'm not sure, but I think the seller said that he could ship it to me. In these small villages, no one seems to speak English. I sure wish Mario was here."

"I bet you do." Jules giggled and fluttered her eyes.

"Well, after you make a decision, I have something to tell you, all of you. I'm going to see if there are enough chairs for us in that little sidewalk café over there. Meet me over there as soon as you can."

Diana looked up at me for the first time since I arrived at the antique section. Her eyes said it all. She didn't really need to speak, but she did. "What's up, Marnie?"

"It's him," I whispered.

She stared at me for a second and then nodded. "I'll be right there."

Up until that moment, I had not realized how safe I had felt with Mario around. Not that he would be able to stave off the Mafia if they attacked, but he was a man, and like it or not, the males of our species do sport a few characteristics we females do not have. He was younger than most of us. He was definitely stronger, and he knew the language and the culture. Our handsome Italian also knew people all over everywhere, and that came in handy quite often during the sometimes bizarre journey.

"Okay, girls," I began after everyone attempted to pull their chairs close to the tiny table. "Our friend or foe—we don't actually know which as yet —in the red beret is standing back there amongst that beautiful pottery."

Lyn gasped and placed her hand on her chest this time.

"You knew that, Lyn," I said, surprised at her action.

"I know, but just to hear it said openly frightens me all over again."

Jules spoke up. "I say, why don't we just march ourselves right over there and ask that guy why he's following us? He wouldn't do us any harm in such a public place."

"I don't know," said Annie, a negative expression filling her usually pleasant countenance.

"Yeah," said Suzanne. "I don't know why, but I have a check in my spirit."

"Well, as Diana mentioned a few minutes ago, no one seems to speak English around here, and I know d'Corsa doesn't because he didn't understand a word I said in the airport restroom. We might have a bit of difficulty confronting him."

"That's true," said Diana.

"I guess so," said Jules. "Wouldn't do much good to ask him any questions."

"And it might just upset him enough to do worse than he planned," added Lyn.

"So, do we just ignore him and enjoy our shopping?" Christmas smiled, knowing her idea would be vetoed.

"I don't see how I can enjoy anything knowing he's right behind us," replied Lyn.

Diana gazed at Lyn, her expression filled with compassion. I knew what she was thinking. Lyn had loved every minute of our days in the enchanted garden where peace and tranquility reigned supreme. Like the rest of us, she had floated around as if in a dream. And now, here she was, back at square one.

After a surprisingly delicious lunch of the local fare, we unanimously decided to hop on our bicycles and head back to the enchanted garden. The d'Corsa look-alike had evidently admired the pottery as long as he could stand it and had chosen another more clandestine spot to watch his prey . . . . us. We didn't see him again, and later we couldn't decide if that was good news or bad.

Angelica served dishes that night that can't be described. Each meal got better and better. And I think it was the only night of our journey that the seven of us said goodnight after dessert and found our way to our rooms just after dark. Whether it was the food or the bicycle ride or the stress of seeing d'Corsa again, I do not know. Either way, we were wiped out.

Now, I have friends—a couple of the sisters and others—who always look to see what time it is when they wake up during the night. I don't do that because I can't imagine why it matters what time it is just as long as I go back to sleep. Nevertheless, I did check the last time I got up to go to the bathroom because I was so tired from thinking about Peeping Tom's appearance in the market that day that I thought it might be interesting to know how much I hadn't slept. It was four a.m.

After my brief visit to the bathroom, I decided that a bit of fresh Tuscan air might help me to sleep, and so I ventured out onto the patio, tying my thin cotton robe about me as I went. Not only was the air fresh and warm and wonderful, the scent of the rose garden below rose up to bless my senses and carry me away like the Calgon commercial. Just as I was thinking my stress was washed away and I was ready to crawl back between my one-thousand-count Egyptian cotton sheets, a loud rattling noise interrupted my thoughts. I couldn't imagine what it was because never in my life have I slept in a place that was so utterly devoid of noise. The only thing, other than music, I had heard in days was the chirping of birds and insects as I lay in the silky grass and dreamed the sweet dreams of a happily aging woman.

Pausing a few moments, awaiting more noise to alert me if something was awry, my thoughts turned to Pete and how much I missed him. Traveling together had always been our favorite hobby, and there I was in romantic Tuscany without my own true love.

The noise I heard to let me know something was awry startled me out of my sweet reverie and frightened me half to death. It sounded as if a person unfamiliar with our lovely villa was walking through the pitch dark kitchen and accidentally knocked all the pots and pans onto the tile floor. From that fairly benign point, the circumstances of those wee hours of the morning went downhill fast.

Someone screamed. I knew it wasn't one of the sisters because it was obviously an Italian scream accompanied by said language going a mile a minute. By the time my feet hit the floor at the bottom of the stairs, I knew it was Angelica, and I knew that my premise was correct. Someone actually *had* knocked pots and pans onto the floor, and Angelica, rather than being afraid, was terribly angry that anyone had presumed to disturb her personal domain.

"Did you see anyone, Angelica?" Somehow, the plump little cook always understood what Christmas said and vice versa.

By that time, each of the seven had arrived in the kitchen as well as Pisa and the two yellow cats that kept mice away from the villa and sometimes settled peacefully into our laps when they felt like it. We all awaited Angelica's reply with eyes wide open and mouths the same.

Like all Italians, Angelica always spoke as much with her arms and hands as with her mouth. But that night, it seemed to be a race as to which could move the fastest, hands or mouth. As Christmas squinted her eyes—the better to understand, I guess—even I was able to translate a few words. Angelica clearly positioned a hat on her head and indicated the number two by holding up two fingers. Next, she let us know that the two were men; however, I must decline to record the clue she so visibly gave us.

It was just as Christmas turned from Angelica to us huddled sisters that I realized what our upset little cook was saying. Only then did I understand that she had pointed to an apple when she positioned the imaginary hat on her head and the apple was red, and that meant the man had a red hat on his head. This time, I was the one who nearly fainted. Lyn was blissfully ignorant, not having understood one iota of Angelica's sign language.

Christmas looked at my face and saw that I knew. "It was him, right?"

"Yes, I think so."

"Come on, let's go get him," said Jules. "I'm tired of this guy messing up our vacation. Which way did he go?"

Christmas spoke and motioned to Angelica to which the cook pointed towards the outside entrance to the kitchen. One after the other, the seven of us plus Angelica, Pisa and the two yellow cats pushed through the door and scurried out to the driveway where we saw red taillights way down the driveway that led to the main road.

I looked at the bicycles leaning on the side of the garage.

"Won't work, Marn," said Suzanne somberly. "Not even Jules could ride a bicycle fast enough to catch a truck."

"Scusi, scusi!" I was amazed at Pisa's excitement. The little waif had
hardly said a word since we arrived. She motioned with her hand for us to
follow her.

As I arrived at the place Pisa stood, happily patting the seat of a medium-
sized motorcycle of European make, I hoped she didn't mean what I
thought she meant. "What's she saying, girls?"

Diana spoke up for the first time that starry night. "I have a feeling
she's offering her motorcycle so that *someone* can chase the burglars."

Her insinuation led me to believe that she would definitely *not* be the
chaser.

We all just stood there staring at the seat of the motorbike where Pisa's
hand was making a rhythmic little drumming sound.

"Christmas," I said, "can you drive this thing? If you can drive, I can sit
on the back with my arms around your waist."

"You sure, Marnie? I've never seen you ride a motorcycle," said Lyn,
sick with worry.

"Sure, I can. Pete and I used to ride around on Sunday afternoons in
Chapel Hill. He drove and I sat on the back."

"When was that, Marn?" Suzanne didn't look too hopeful about my
cycling abilities.

"1966."

My friends looked at me and like sextuplets, each created the same
identical frown.

"Christmas," I took up where I left off, "can you drive this thing or not?"

"I think so. I mow my yard at the ranch back in Texas with a tractor-
like thingy. I guess I could drive this."

"Well, get on. That man is going to be so far ahead of us we'll never see the
red beret, and if we lose him now, we'll have no proof he's done anything."

The Bible says, I think, that God's eyes run to and fro throughout the
earth and that's exactly what Angelica's were doing while we discussed the
situation. She was still angry that someone had invaded her territory, but
confusion soon overcame her anger.

Just before Christmas threw her long right leg over the bike, Jules
spoke up rather hastily. "Don't, Christmas. I'll drive. My boys taught me

how when they were teenagers."

"You're more updated than Marn," said Suzanne. "At least we're up to the nineties."

"The man is getting away, y'all!" Lyn's scream scared us back to reality. She was seldom loud, but when she was loud, she was *very* loud.

Annie had been as quiet as the cats. "Uhm, when and if you catch up with d'Corsa, what are you going to do?"

Christmas smiled. "Yeah, you gonna place him under citizen's arrest? Do they have that in Italy?"

That was one thing I hadn't thought of during all my pondering. What *would* I do if we caught him? I had no weapon of any sort although Pete had begged me to buy a tiny little pistol when we arrived in Italy for our protection under whatever circumstances we might find ourselves. That night would have been a good time to have it if for nothing but to prove to d'Corsa we women meant business. He had no right to be following us in the first place and in the second place, he certainly had no right to break into our peaceful home away from home.

"You know," I said while struggling to settle my sixty-four-year-old caboose onto a strip of padding about six inches wide, "I wonder why he broke into the house?"

At that pensive moment, Jules shoved the pedal to the metal, and we shot out of our circle of friends like a clown out of a cannon at the circus. It's a good thing Jules is so small that my arms might have made two trips around her waist because I was able to lock my fingers together and hold on tight. We zoomed away into the night like Batman and Robin, ready to meet our foe.

Night is dark in rural Tuscany. I couldn't help but think that we have lights most everywhere in America, even in the country. I was glad that dawn was coming soon. I had no idea how much time we had wasted after Pisa so gladly offered the bike, but I naturally assumed about thirty minutes had passed since the break-in, possibly more.

"Do you think we can catch him?" I had to scream in Jules's ear for her to hear me over the roar.

"Sure we can. That truck sounded pretty old to me and this bike is fast."

The tone of Jules's voice encouraged me so much I began to feel blithe-ly light and almost happy. I decided then and there to sit back and enjoy the ride. When would I ever again have the opportunity to see the sun rise over Tuscany from the back of a speeding motorcycle?

Just as an enormous ball of fire began to beam its radiant light over grape-filled vineyards and glistening olive groves, Jules yelled, "There's the truck! See it, Marn?"

I couldn't see the truck. My eyes were so affected by the fireball that I saw suns everywhere I turned. One would have thought Jules had driven that motorcycle into another galaxy.

"Giddy up!" I shouted, poking Jules slightly in the ribs. "Don't let him get away!"

"Hold on!" she yelled, speeding up more than I thought we could.

Did you see the movie, *Secretariat?* Well, it was like that. It looked as if we were falling way behind, but when Jules gunned the motor, it was as if Ron Turcoutte, the jockey, had urged Secretariat into full speed ahead, and within a few exhilarating minutes, we were on d'Corsa's tail instead of the other way around.

And then we passed him. "Why did you do that?" I had learned I did-n't have to yell quite so loud in Jules's ear.

"I'm going to block him so he'll have to stop!"

"Good idea!"

Jules slowed the bike down, guiding it from one side of the road to the other as the getaway truck tried to go the other way, like in the movies. Strange, but it was there on the highway in the truck's headlights with the Tuscan sun now in full view that I remembered that Jules and I were still wearing our sleeping attire. Thankfully for Jules, she bedded her slender body down in clothing akin to sweat pants and T-shirt while I, on the other hand, wore my cotton gown and robe, the one I bought just for Italy. I guess one might say I was getting the most out of my money, so I decided not to worry about that either if I could just keep my thighs from showing.

Pete never had the luxury of becoming a Boy Scout in his youth, but he must have been born an Eagle Scout because he is always prepared. And he, being my concerned husband, tries his best to help me be prepared, but this time, I wasn't. Neither was Jules. It never crossed our minds that a vehicle might come from the frontal direction towards us and the truck, but that's exactly what happened.

In the split second that she saw the van coming, Jules shouted, "Oops! Hold on, Marn!"

I'm still thanking God that I didn't see it. But frankly, if your own driver says, "Oops!" one certainly expects something milder than a head-on collision. To this day, I have no idea how Jules navigated that little bike so that we ended up flying over a fence into a sheep pasture instead of hitting either the truck or the van. All I could say when she stood over me asking if I was alright, was, "Wow."

She said, "Guess what, Marn?"

"Ugh?" I sort of groaned, I think, feeling of my head to see if there were any bumps while Jules tried to pull me to my unstable feet.

"Mario was driving the van!" Jules's happy face was lovely, framed against the blue Tuscan sky in all its glory.

"What about d'Corsa? Did he get away?"

"Yeah, I'm sorry. After our bike left the road, he wheeled around the van and sped out of sight."

"Don't worry about him," said Mario, strolling up to my landing spot as if nothing had happened. "I got the license of the truck and called the authorities. He will be picked up before long. How are you, my friends?" He smiled and the Tuscan sun shown brighter.

"Okay, I guess." Jules had pulled me to a sitting position. By then, every bone and muscle in my body was sending pain signals to my brain. Jules just looked as if she had been riding her horse for an hour or two, breathing a bit fast but not in the least bit injured or distraught.

Mario seemed to express no surprise whatsoever regarding the predicament he had found us in. "Let me help you stand, Marnie." From the back, he put one tanned arm under my elbows and the other around my waist. *Oh, Pete,* I thought, *so glad you're not here to see this.*

"I'm sure you have had enough excitement for one day," said our Italian friend with his usual smile.

"You would be correct in that assessment," I said.

Jules flipped out her cell phone. "It's only . . . wow, 6:30 a.m. and look what we've accomplished."

I laughed, and Mario joined in. "Oh," I groaned, "don't say anything funny. It makes me hurt to laugh."

"A merry heart doeth good like medicine," quoted Jules.

Mario helped us into the van, saying he had already sent for a garage to pick up the motorbike.

"Oh, no!" Jules sudden exclamation startled me.

"What's wrong now?" I leaned my head back on the seat and closed my eyes. I might never get over this trip to Italy.

"I'll have to pay Pisa for the bike. I'm sure it's in bad shape, right, Mario?"

"Si, it does look bad, but the bike is not Pisa's."

"It isn't?" Jules glanced at Mario from the front passenger seat.

"No, it belongs to the property as an amenity for the guests' enjoyment."

"Well, that's good," I muttered. "We sure enjoyed it. For a little while, anyway."

"We did, didn't we?" Jules turned around and grinned at me.

"I would like to ask why you ladies were on a motorcycle at 6:00 a.m. chasing a truck with your night clothing on, but I will hold my questions until you are rested and we are reunited with your friends."

The path to the villa was now in sight. I could hardly wait. I hoped I wasn't too dirty to get back in bed. My mind began to wander. "Will they call us in to testify, Mario?" I grimaced. My back had always given me problems. I wondered how I was going to explain this to my chiropractor.

"I am sure you will be questioned but, hopefully, not interrogated." He chuckled and glanced in the rearview mirror.

"You're funny," I replied with only a hint of sarcasm.

Diana's blonde hair was glowing in the morning sun. She sat regally in a cushioned lawn chair on the stone patio. Mario turned the switch to the off position and jumped out of the van. I stifled a laugh. He reminded me of seven lords a' leaping. Evidently, he forgot Jules and me in lieu of the lovely Diana. Feeling a bit down and concerned that I might not be able to move the remainder of our vacation in Italy, I couldn't decide whether to try to get out of the van or to sit there all day waiting for Mario to remember me. Thankfully, Jules did not forget her injured friend and somehow removed me from the very high off-the-ground vehicle.

One by one, the seven sisters gathered around Diana's throne on the patio. Christmas called for Angelica and Pisa, and they hurried out to meet us, cats at their heels.

"What happened to the bike?" Christmas's questions always seem so casual no matter what's going on.

"Why are you with Mario?" Suzanne had finally given up doing the cross-eyed thing. Her eyes would have never straightened up after that trip.

Annie and Lyn stood silently by, awaiting our explanations with their usual patience. Angelica was muttering something, but I didn't know what. Pisa stood half hidden by Angelica's ample girth. I looked at them all, and for one of the first times in all my entire life, I publicly broke down in tears.

"Aw, Marn," cooed Suzanne.

Lyn threw her anointed arms around me and hugged tight. I rested my head on her shoulder and sobbed for a minute or two. Finally, I caught my breath.

"I'm just too tired and in too much pain to explain," I said. "Jules can tell you the story, I'm sure." I turned to Jules who was patting my shoulder. "Don't forget the sunrise. That was the best part."

"I won't," promised Jules, smiling at the memory.

Lyn and Suzanne helped me up the stairs and into my wonderful sleep wonder bed. I didn't even have to change clothes, dressed as I was in my lovely cotton nightgown. I don't remember another minute of that day. I do hope someone took pictures.

Chapter Thirteen

FROM WHAT I'VE HEARD, all my friends took long naps that day including Mario. He conked out on the daybed on the sleeping porch (a nice Southern concept, I must say) while the others took to their rooms. Suzanne said they spent the remainder of the day just hanging out in several of our favorite spots, talking and speculating about our, by then, notorious burglar and his unfathomable motive for stalking us for days on end and then breaking into our private abode.

The morning following our day of rest and reflection, I painfully eased my aching body down the stairs, one step at a time. When I finally hit bottom, I was surprised to find that the furniture had been rearranged. A lovely little settee—much like the one Diana wanted at the market—had been removed from its precise habitation in the hallway at the bottom of the stairs.

"Y'all," I said, walking into the dining room where the others had already gathered for breakfast, "who rearranged the furniture?"

"What do you mean?" Diana was bringing her teacup to her mouth as she spoke.

"That lovely little pecan settee with the jacquard cushion, it's been moved." I took the empty seat beside Annie and reached over to give her a quick hug.

Italian coffee is good. Don't let anyone tell you French Roast is better. I closed my eyes for a second or two, enjoying the pleasure of the hot liquid seeping down my throat and into all the nooks and crannies of my throbbing body.

Angelica brought more hot eggs and sausages and placed them on the table in front of me. Smiling and humming what I figured was an Italian tune, she looked at me and said, "Buon giorno, signora Marnie!"

"Buon giorno, Angelica," I replied in turn, casting a painful smile in her direction. My face had caught the full essence of the field in which Jules and I had landed the day before and I was left looking pretty much like I did the time I fell on my face in an asphalt parking lot when I had braces on my teeth. Angelica gently placed her hands on both my cheeks and tearfully said something I knew in my heart was full of compassion.

"I think she thinks you should go to a doctor, Marnie." Christmas was sitting on my left, and her soft voice came in strong and clear.

I tried my best to assure Angelica that I would be fine but I could tell by her hovering like a mother hen and cackling all the while that she was not convinced.

I was just about to ask Christmas to ask Angelica about the missing settee when our muttering little cook walked over to the beautifully painted china cabinet and opened a drawer. *"Mama mia! Che macello!"* Her arms were flailing all over the place.

"What's wrong?" Christmas was already at Angelica's side. She looked back at us. "I think she's saying that something is missing, and I'm pretty sure it's the silver flatware."

"Christmas, ask her if she moved the settee that was in the hallway." My wheels had started turning.

Christmas took Angelica by the arm and almost had to pull her out of the dining room and into the hallway. I followed as quickly as I could, considering the effect my wounds were having on my aging body. The others nervously awaited the verdict.

Angelica took one look at the empty spot where the settee was supposed to be and screamed, *"Mama mia!"* again and again.

While staring at the distraught cook—my weak knees trembling a bit—I came up with a plan. "Girls," I said, returning to the dining room, "let's go to our rooms to see if anything personal is missing while Angelica and Pisa search the house. We'll meet back in the living room in about fifteen minutes."

The sound of chairs scuffling and glasses clinking added to the din still coming from the hallway where Angelica was evidently explaining to Pisa what had happened. Pisa looked as if she might lean a little too far and fall on the floor. Her lovely dark eyes were popping somewhat.

As each of us scuttled to our assignments, I struggled back up the stairs to my cozy room which I now knew had been desecrated by an evil presence. Just as I was coming to a conclusion about how personally invasive burglary is, I saw Suzanne rushing down the hall towards me, Jules right behind. I guess it had taken me longer than I thought to climb the stairs.

"My pretty pendant is gone, the one Butch gave me for our anniversary!" Not one to tear up about any old thing, Suzanne's tear-filled eyes were about to overflow.

"What about you, Jules?"

"I didn't think I had anything worth stealing, but some of my things are gone as well. I brought the turquoise jewelry I got from the Inuit chief last year."

"Come on in my room while I look around." They followed me into my room and sat on the beautifully made bed while I searched. I couldn't help but wonder when Pisa made the bed. I thought she had been downstairs the whole time. That girl was amazing.

"Uh, oh. The Star of David necklace I bought in Israel is gone. It didn't cost much money, but it's worth a lot to me." Sadly, I continued my search. "Oh, no!"

"What? What?" Jules and Suzanne echoed one another.

"My camera! Pete gave it to me last Christmas, and it's a really nice camera for an amateur." I couldn't help but groan and for a lot of reasons.

"Forget the camera, Marn," Suzanne retorted, "your SD card is what matters!"

"Ugh!!!! My pictures of Rome and Venice and Florence and worse than that, the enchanted garden!"

"Let's pray," said Lyn who was standing in the doorway watching our distressing discovery.

And so we did. Lyn called down the corridor for the others who were already making their way towards my room from which came all the noise. Each of us was missing at least one important, if not valuable, piece of jewelry as well as electronic equipment and even a cell phone which belonged to Christmas. I had mine because I had dozed off the night of the burglary while Skyping with Pete, and the phone ended up under my pillow.

After our prayers, my defiled room was totally restored to its original peace and purity. When I shared that with my friends, we quickly decided that we should pray in each one's bedroom as well. No sense leaving some little demon lurking around. And so we did. And after we prayed in the last room, Diana's, the seven of us sat in silence for quite a while, enjoying the peace our prayers had created. It was when I saw Christmas close her eyes and nod that my brain went back to "think" mode, and I realized that not only were material things missing but humans as well.

"Where is Mario?"

"Yeah, where is that hunk?" Jules giggled, of course.

Blushing, Diana replied, "He drove to Florence late last night. Something about the police report he needed to add."

Diana's blush darkened into alizarin crimson when she realized that she had admitted that Mario left "late" last night and she was the only one who knew about it. Everyone was staring at her as if she were Lady Chatterley.

"So, tell us what's going on with you two." I smiled and tickled her foot.

"Yeah, your public wants to know." I'll be darned if Suzanne didn't cross her eyes again.

"There really isn't anything to tell," said Diana, her blush now deepening from pinky alizarin to pure dark red. She quickly pulled the soft aqua scarf from her neck and covered her face.

"Sure, there isn't." Christmas was enjoying Diana's misery. One didn't normally get Diana's goat as they say.

"Come on, girl," prodded Jules. "Tell it like it is."

Diana sighed so deeply, I saw her chest heave up and down. "Okay, you win."

"Yippee!" Christmas clapped her hands.

"I'll have to admit that Mario and I are . . . well, I guess you'd say we're interested in one another."

"That's the understatement of the year," I said. "You'll have to do better than that."

Our Diana really looked at us for the first time since the beginning of the embarrassing conversation, smiles all over her face that she couldn't seem to control. "I really like him. And I believe he likes me just as much."

"Of course, he does," said Lyn. "That's obvious."

"Tell us more." I struggled to pull myself up a little, settling my painful back against the lovely walnut headboard.

Each of us needed to make ourselves more comfortable it seemed. Seven women over fifty on a double bed was a lot of human flesh. After a few seconds of moving and heaving and a little grunting, we were all settled and ready for Diana's tell-all.

Now, I must say here that it doesn't take as long for Diana to tell a story as it does me. In fact, I could see that she was searching for the quickest way to get it told without taking all day and without sharing too much.

"I really can't explain how I feel about him. He's intelligent. He's kind and considerate and very polite."

"And he's a hunk," Jules interjected.

"Yes, he is," Diana agreed, laughing with us all.

"I've never had so much in common with anyone in my entire life. We talk for hours and never run out of topics. He's conservative. At least, if he were American, he'd be considered conservative. Not sure what you call it in Italian."

"That's good," I said, thrilled she wasn't hooked up with some far left-wing communist.

"Has he been married?" We could always depend on Annie to get to the point.

"Yes, he has. He's been divorced for five years. He has two married children, a boy and a girl who live in Rome."

"Wait a minute." I interrupted this time. "I thought Catholics couldn't get divorced, particularly Italian Catholics. They have the Pope in residence to keep them straight."

"I don't know, Marnie. I didn't get into all that with him." Diana's tone sounded as if she didn't want to get into it with me either.

"Alrighty then," I said, "let's move on."

"That's about it, I guess. We love being together, and I cannot bear the thought of leaving Italy in a few days." Sweet tears perched on the brim of Diana's blue eyes. Her lips quivered a little as Lyn handed her a tissue.

I quickly put it all together. "You're in love, did you know that?"

Diana burst into tears. "I thought so but I wasn't sure."

Suzanne said, "Well, you are. You have all the signs. That's the way I used to talk about Butch."

Each of us gazed at Diana for a few moments, probably reflecting back over many years to seasons of true love. I missed Pete so bad it made my back hurt worse.

"Oh, what am I going to do, girls? I can't live in Italy," she moaned.

"Of course, you can," said Christmas who had lived most everywhere in her lifetime.

"But how will I make a living? I can't even speak Italian!"

We seriously pondered Diana's query for a few moments while she carefully blotted her eyes.

"There's another very important issue to consider, girls. Mario hasn't proposed. I'm sure he loves me, but with what I've heard about Italian men, I don't know if he wants to marry me and settle down to a normal life. But since Mario came into my life, it's been as if I'm living in a dream, and perhaps I am. Perhaps it is just a dream."

"No, it isn't." We were shocked to hear Annie speak, particularly so emphatically. Everyone turned to listen.

I guess she didn't have anything else to say. Annie had made her point. She knows Diana better than anyone, so we had no doubt Annie was on target. Neither did Diana. "Thank you," she whispered.

Finally, Diana's chest heaved a sigh and said, "Okay, girls, enough of this. Now, I'm ruining our vacation." She uttered a rather sad chuckle.

"No, you're not," said Lyn, pulling Diana into her arms.

"Of course not," said Jules. "I suggest that we just go with the flow and see what happens. I always say there's no sense in making decisions before the last minute."

"I think I hear the lunch bell ringing," said Suzanne.

"The lunch bell doesn't ring," replied Christmas. "We have lunch on our own, remember?"

"Yes, but I'm sure that was the bell. I just love bells. I have lots of pictures of cow bells in Switzerland from when I vacationed there with my cousin."

At that moment, Pisa knocked softly on the door frame, looking as if she had something to say and didn't know how to say it. I guess she made a quick decision and thought it best to use sign language. Obviously pretending she had an eating utensil in her hand, she dipped it in the air and brought it to her mouth. Then she chewed, swallowed and gave us a big smile.

"It really was the lunch bell," I mused.

"I told you, Marn."

"Angelica must have decided we needed a good lunch and I, for one, am very thankful." Annie pushed herself up and carefully dismounted the high bed.

"Me, too. For some reason, I'm starving." Jules held her stomach with one hand and pulled me up with the other. It was harder than she thought.

"Ohhhh," I groaned. "I wish our enchanted garden had an elevator."

"No complaining, Marnie, remember our rule?" Diana blew her nose and sighed again.

"Sorry," I said. "But you'll have to admit that I'm rather handicapped at the moment."

"Yes, you are, but we will help you down the stairs." Diana put her arm around my back and led me to the stairs.

"Come on, Marn. You can do it." Jules took the stairs two at a time, laughing all the way.

The dining room table looked as if the entire region of Tuscany had been invited to lunch at our enchanted garden. Angelica had outdone herself, and no one was more pleased than seven American women who were now totally involved in a very legitimate Italian romance as well as a burglary, not to mention a stalker situation.

"I'm going to weigh a ton by the time I get home," I remarked, preparing to take the last bite of Angelica's absolutely luscious double chocolate cake. Remember the movie, *Chocolat?* That movie put five pounds on me, I'm sure.

"I'm going to take a walk," said Diana pushing back from the table.

"Want company?" asked Annie, careful to give Diana space that day.

"No, I don't think so. I need to think."

I needed to write, and so did Suzanne. We agreed to meet on the patio by the rose garden where our prose would be stimulated by the sweet smelling rose. No rhyme intended.

Even with so many issues left unresolved, it was a peaceful afternoon. The magic of our enchanted garden weaved its way into our souls as the gentle breezes of Tuscany wrapped our bodies in warm embrace.

Suzanne and I found ourselves nodding off from time to time, and we didn't even care. We smiled at one another and looked back at our journals, knowing it wouldn't matter in the least if we didn't write a single word.

After at least an hour of doing pretty much nothing, Suzanne looked over at me and smiled. "Marn, do you think God cares if we're Catholic or Protestant? People on both sides are pretty adamant about it, you know."

I looked up into the radiant blue sky. One lone bird was circling. As I watched, he flew off towards the barn and perched on a rusty old weather-vane. Christmas said the birds that live there were doves. She's a birdwatcher.

"Nope. I don't think He cares one iota. And at this point in my life, I don't care either."

Suzanne nodded. "I know what you mean. Each group—even groups within groups—is constantly arguing about how *right* they are. In my humble opinion, I think it's more a matter of how *wrong* we are."

"How so?"

The dove left his lookout on the weathervane and soared up into the blue, coming again to circle high above our place in the rose garden. I wondered if the dove was a sign of some sort. Birds can be, you know, especially doves.

"Well, when you think of how big God is and how totally incomprehensible to our human understanding, and then you think of how many different religions, even denominations, are trying to figure Him out, I figure they all have to be much more wrong than right."

"Hmm, I see."

Suzanne let that sink in and then she asked, "Do you think Mario will propose to Diana before we leave Italy?"

"What does that have to do with religions?"

"Nothing. I just wondered what you thought." Suzanne smiled and lifted her eyebrows up and down. I was glad she had acquired a safer quirk.

"You know, it *could* have something to do with religions."

"Yeah?" Suzanne had now spotted the bird and was craning her neck to watch his unusual flight pattern.

"Diana is Protestant. Mario is Catholic. *Problemo.*"

She turned from the bird to me. "Oh, great, another issue to resolve."

"Now that I think about it, that's the one issue Diana didn't mention this morning. She didn't say if she and Mario were spiritually compatible, and knowing Diana, that's the most important thing. I wonder if they've discussed it."

"Surely, they have," said Suzanne.

Before we could discuss it any further, steps were heard on the flagstone path coming from the main house. In a moment, Christmas appeared, all smiley and happy. "Mario is back, and you're summoned to the castle."

"I'm glad he's back, but do we have to leave our little spot of heaven now? We'll see him at dinner." Suzanne's tone was almost pleading.

"A summons is a summons, Suze. Mine is not to reason why."

"Alright. Pull me up."

It was a lot harder to pull *me* up, but with both of them pulling, I finally made it.

In retrospect, I think Mario was happier to be back with us than we were to see him on that warm late afternoon. Except for the day before when everyone slept so much, he had been away for days. His happiness in being united with us six as well as Diana caused me to admire his character even more, and I planned to tell him so. If I see something nice in someone, I make it a rule to let that person know it. I believe some folks are literally dying from lack of affirmation.

We scattered about the living room and made ourselves comfortable in the lovely down-filled sofas and chairs. Like Goldilocks's bed, they seemed to have been made "just right" to fit our various-sized torsos. Each time I sat in one, it was all I could do to stay awake, and I'm not normally a daytime sleeper. Neither am I a nighttime sleeper.

Mario couldn't keep his eyes off Diana . . . or his hands. For the first time since the relationship budded, she allowed him to hold her hand in public. Of course, we were not public in the true sense, but we were not totally private either. She had dressed especially for him, I could tell. Usually in pants, that day Diana wore a soft flowing white skirt that stopped just above her slender ankles to show off the loveliest pair of Italian-made turquoise sandals I've ever seen. Not that I've seen a lot of Italian sandals, but these were particularly beautiful and showed off her newly acquired pedicure quite nicely. Her top was made of the same soft flowing fabric in that color of sea blue that Diana wears so well. She wore long dangling earrings made of twinkling crystals and tiny white bracelets. The two of them together on the sofa were quite a sight to behold, sort of like Carlos of Il Divo and Princess Diana.

"We're glad you're back, Mario," said Annie.

"Yeah, it hasn't been the same without you." Christmas smiled, rubbing the yellow cat who had taken a seat in her lap. We sometimes call Christmas the Cat Lady because she once rescued seventy-five strays and found homes for them. We were so proud of her.

"So," said Jules, "did the cops find the burglar? I hope he's behind bars."

"Was it Lucien d'Corsa?" I so hoped my artist hadn't fallen off the pedestal I'd placed him on.

We all started talking at once, everyone but Diana, asking so many questions the noise sounded like the gaggle of geese that now followed Christmas around the estate. A friendly neighboring farmer, signor Alberto, had given the orphans to Christmas to raise, and she had done such a good job that the goslings thought she was their mother. Thankfully, she didn't allow them in the house. Now that I think about it, Angelica was the one who vetoed that idea. Had she not, the baby goslings might have slept in the bed with Christmas and the cats.

Diana finally held up her bejeweled hand which was obviously a signal for all of us to quieten down so Mario could speak. When the hand descended to rest on Mario's knee, I didn't know what to think. Was this *our* Diana? It's really hard to focus when there's so much going on.

That wonderful Italian smile enveloped us all as Mario began his report. "*Mi bella* signoras, you have added something that was missing in my life—excitement! I might change my occupation to private investigator after this mystery is solved."

Each of us joined in the laughter and the sweet camaraderie of good friends.

"I'm sure you'd make a good PI." Diana smiled, and I noticed she squeezed his hand. Or perhaps he squeezed hers; I'm not quite sure.

"I am very happy to announce that my friend, Inspector Franco, was able to get the message out in time for our local police to pull the truck over when Panzinni drove through the village. He was taken to Firenze and now temporarily resides in jail along with his accomplice. All the stolen items have been retrieved due to the quick response of the village police. Your jewelry and camera are being held in Florence along with the missing household items."

Simultaneously, we clapped our hands and cheered. Finally, we could enjoy our vacation without the stress of wondering if we were being watched all the time as well as the fear of the unknown which is a terrible fear to live with as FDR sort of said.

"So what's next?" The cat rolled over for Christmas to scratch his belly. Or hers, I never can tell with cats.

"Will there be a trial?" Suzanne was way ahead of me.

"First of all, the inspector will schedule a . . . ah . . . lineup, I think you call it in America?"

"Yes, I've seen them in movies," said Suzanne, "but not in real life. I just hate it when they choose the wrong person."

"Me, too," I said. "It makes everything so complicated."

Evidently, Diana had worked her thoughts away from Mario a few moments to sense something I hadn't. "Sounds as if we will be the ones choosing from the lineup." She glanced at Mario, her eyes questioning his.

"Si. Inspector Franco asked that I deliver all of you to the station in Florence next Tuesday at 10:00 a.m."

All of us seemed to be in shock, but Lyn, longing for Pops and her own bed, was the one to speak out. "But . . . but, we're leaving Tuscany Friday and flying from Rome on Sunday."

"Not," said Christmas, smiling at the cat.

"Wow, what will my principal say?" Our Jules looked stricken.

"Don't you think he'll give you a leave of absence?" replied Diana. "Certainly, this is an educational journey. It has been for me." Diana managed a laugh while the rest of us pondered Jules's quandary.

"Maybe," answered Jules, sounding quite iffy.

The year before our trip, Suzanne had begun to teach English as a second language outside the public school system just so she could be ready to go someplace when the opportunity arose. Butch liked to travel, too, so her decision worked out well for everyone, seven sisters included.

Annie and Diana had finally come to the place in their development business where they could work most anyplace in the world that had an internet connection. It was a freedom they celebrated every day of their lives. Of course, Diana seemed pretty happy about the delay in getting back to the States. More time with Mario was exactly what she had been praying for.

As for me, Pete was managing all our business affairs, and I could write anywhere if it wasn't too hot. What more could a writer desire than an enchanted garden to inspire words that touch the heart of one's readers? I would miss Pete terribly—as well as my children and grandchildren—that was for sure, but with all the communication devices we traveled with, I could see and talk to them every day.

Lyn began to cry. "Oh, I just can't bear it. I talked to Pops last night, and he was so happy that I'd be back home Sunday night. This will break his heart. And he'll drive the children crazy."

Each of us, including Mario, gazed at Lyn with eyes filled with compassion. There seemed to be nothing we could say that would alleviate the pain she bore.

Christmas's countenance suddenly lit up. "What if we invite Pops to our enchanted garden?"

Lyn wiped her eyes and let out a sigh. "You've lost your mind, Christmas. The only enchanted garden Pops is ever going to visit is his own forty acres, full of hay and cows and pigs and stray dogs."

My own input wasn't too helpful either. "Surely, we can figure something out."

"Mario," said Diana, "does Inspector Franco really need Lyn? My goodness, there are seven of us. Certainly, one witness less wouldn't change anything. At first, it was just Marnie and Lyn, and then Suzanne, but we all saw d'Corsa in the market that day. I think I could identify him easily, even without the red beret."

"Hmm," said Annie, finally joining in. "That's right. I'm sure I'd recognize him. I stared at him for a long time when he wasn't looking at us."

Lyn looked at Mario, hope written all over her face.

"It sounds like a good idea, but I cannot say for sure. I will call Franco and ask."

"Oh, please do," begged Lyn. "Ask him to *pleeeeease* let me go. I just have to get back to Pops."

My friend was in great distress. When Mario went on to give us more details of what would be expected of us at the lineup, Lyn got up and hurried out of the room and up the stairs. After much pulling and pushing to get myself out of the chair, I followed her.

"Lyn, we've got to talk." I sat down on the edge of the bed on which she had thrown herself. I could tell she wasn't going to do much talking; sobbing was more like it.

"Listen, now. Mario is going to do everything he can to get you back to Pops on time. But Lyn, if the inspector says you will have to stay, you'll just have to stay, and that's all there is to it. You can handle it; I know you can. Remember that time we went to Phoenix? And the time we attended that conference in Denver?"

"But . . . ." She paused to blow her nose. "They were short trips compared to this. We've been gone forever!"

"I know; I know."

I find it interesting that relationships are so different. Lyn and Pops had been together since the ninth grade and were married long before she was twenty. And except for the times that I took her away, she and Pops had stuck together like glue. I sometimes wonder if it's a temperament thing.

Pete and I have been together since high school as well, but we both like our space and sometimes, lots of it. We communicate throughout the day whether I'm home, at the beach or in a foreign country. Sometimes, he can't remember where I am and calls me just to find out. And if Pete hears anything exciting or otherwise on his XM radio, he calls to tell me about it, knowing I don't keep up as well as he does and he likes to keep me informed.

Anyway, there I was in Italy with a dear, heartbroken friend and no way to comfort her. What to do?

And then the thought came to me as it had over and over again during my lengthening life. The Bible says (and I know this one is right) that Job's best friends were the ones who didn't say anything. They just sat with him on his dung heap. So that's what I did. And so did Annie when she crept into the room. One on either side of the bed, we sat with Lyn until the sun lowered behind the distant olive grove and the dinner bell rang from the kitchen.

Our friend was fast asleep.

Chapter Fourteen

EXCEPT FOR CONCERN OVER LYN'S RELAPSE, the weekend was delightful. She wandered around the grounds like a little lost puppy until Annie finally called Pops to explain our situation and then called Lyn to the phone so he could assure her that he wouldn't die before she got back to North Carolina. He also wouldn't torment the children in his angst. She was much better after that and didn't react too terribly when Mario called us back together to say that Inspector Franco particularly wanted Lyn at the lineup because, other than me, she had seen d'Corsa more than anyone and from the very beginning in the airport.

Mario pulled enough strings with the powers that were to get our tickets changed without charge since we were aiding the Italian police force in a criminal investigation. If we hadn't been so nervous about choosing the guilty person in the lineup, we might have felt rather important. I mean, how many other tourists get to take part in governmental affairs in a foreign country?

When I paint—pictures, not houses—I need lots of space, and I seem to need every utensil in the arts and crafts store. Suzanne, on the other hand, operates quite differently. She continued to take a lot of photographs to paint in the days and years following our journey, but she painted in our enchanted garden as well. Most mornings after breakfast, Suzanne took a child's watercolor palette, a brush or two and a pad of paper in a cloth bag that read, "Keep North Carolina Clean and Green," and happily walked to her spot of the day, carefully chosen the day before. My little pixie-like friend's watercolor impressions of our enchanted garden turned out to be nothing short of extraordinary. Beatrix Potter couldn't have done better. Every area of the estate including cats, dogs, geese and sheep came back to North Carolina ready to be framed and placed in Suzanne's daughter's art gallery. A few times, we painted together with Suzanne giving me tips on painting with watercolors which I loved but wasn't experienced in at all. Oils were my thing, of course. They required much more mess and complications.

"Suzanne," said Diana Sunday evening during dinner, "our day at the village market proved to be so chaotic we never had time to discuss all the pretties we found."

Even though Diana was speaking to Suzanne, it reminded me of something I had been meaning to say. "That's true and I want to go back to that market without what's-his-name on our heels. Anyone want to go tomorrow? We're free women until Tuesday."

My joke didn't go over too well. Lyn put down her fork and stared at me. Thank goodness, she had begun to eat something.

"I want to go back, too," said Diana, "and I hope Suzanne will. I was a bit surprised considering the size of that tiny village, but I went into the cutest little shop that sold hand-made crafts, mostly local, I think. The proprietor spoke some English, and if I understood her correctly, she said they operate like an American consignment shop. She said they have much more business than one would think because of all the villas for rent in the area. Suzanne, I wish you would take some of your watercolors to her. They are as good as anything I saw there and much better than most. And, your close-ups would be a good contrast with all the broad Tuscan landscapes they have now."

Suzanne had been listening intently. "Do you really think my work is comparable?"

"Yes, more than comparable," replied Diana.

We all nodded in agreement. Annie spoke up. "I want to buy a couple, Suzanne. You really captured our little paradise, and to keep it always before me on the wall in my office would be a perfect way to remember our journey."

"Wow. Y'all flatter me. But more than that, you give me the encouragement I need. Thanks." Suzanne smiled and reached over to squeeze Jules's hand.

"That's what we're here for," said Christmas with that twinkle in her eye.

"Oh, this is wonderful," I exclaimed. "Suzanne's artwork in Italy of all places, the art capital of the world!"

"Now, let's not count our chickens before they hatch," warned Suzanne, calming my usual exuberance at one of my sister's great ideas which they so often have.

"Well, what is faith if it's not counting your chickens before they hatch?" Christmas made that deep little chuckle of hers. "From the Book of Marnie, Chapter 1, verse 1, 'Faith is counting your chickens before they hatch.'"

Annie looked my way and smiled. "By the way, Marnie, how's the writing coming along?"

"Actually, my book is almost ready to send to Edie, my editor. You might be surprised to find yourselves in the storyline."

"Oh, Lord." Lyn almost groaned. "What have you done to us now?"

"Think of it this way. You might become famous." I got up and threw my arms about Lyn's sagging shoulders from behind.

"That's the last thing on earth I want to be. Pops would have a fit."

Christmas said, "Yeah, can't you imagine WITN news cameras and media people all over Lyn and Pops's place? Wouldn't that be fun?"

"That part he could handle, couldn't he, Lyn?" I asked. "If I know Pops, he would throw a big pig-picking and put Lyn to work making coleslaw and hushpuppies."

"Yes, as long as I stayed home, he wouldn't care if I was famous."

"I want to travel more," said Diana with a dreamy look on her face. "Paris, London, Timbuktu; I want to go everywhere."

"I bet Mario will take you," teased Christmas. "I think he'd take you anywhere you want to go."

Diana smiled, a little twinkle in her eye this time.

The large lion-faced knockers on the front doors of the villa echoed all through the house as if someone were beating Morse code on a drum.

We glanced at one another with a look that asked, *Who could that be?* Mario had gone to Florence for the day, and Pisa and Angelica were inside the house. Except for the gardener, we didn't know anyone else, and he would have come to the back door.

We waited in silence while Pisa's sprite figure flowed from out of nowhere to the front of the house. The conversation in Italian only lasted a few seconds, and by that time, Christmas had gotten up and walked towards the arched doorway.

"Who is it, Christmas?" asked Annie.

"Just a friend," she replied and kept on walking.

The rest of us looked at each other. "How on earth does Christmas make friends when we haven't even seen anybody to make friends with?" Inwardly, we all asked the same question as Jules.

In another minute or two, we may have all had heart attacks or at least, arrhythmia, had we not gone to see who was at the door. Making an unusual amount of noise, pushing chairs aside and scuffling to get to the living room, the six of us made our way through the large room to the double front doors. And there stood our tall Texan chatting in English with the farmer who gave her the goslings. He was speaking Italian. Pete once had a secretary who married a Hispanic guy and neither one of them could speak the other's language, so I knew that some type of communication was possible. Of course, they got divorced about a year later.

Smiling from head to toe, Christmas introduced us to her friend. "Girls, this is signor Alberto. He owns the property north of our villa."

Alberto nodded happily, greeting us with a cheerful, *"Felice di conoscerti."* We had learned that meant, "Glad to meet you."

I liked him right off the bat. He looked to be about the same age as Christmas and the same height as well. He looked just like someone I'd seen before, but I couldn't quite pull it up. Sometimes, a picture teeters just on the precipice of my memory, awaiting someone or something to click the mouse.

"Won't you come in, signor Alberto?" Diana beckoned him in.

Well, I've seen some interesting things in my life and been in some strange situations, but the next twenty minutes might have topped them all. One lone Italian man who spoke not one word of English other than *hello* and *goodbye* carried on a conversation with seven women who spoke only the basic rudiments of Italian such as, "Where is the restroom?" and I've even forgotten that now.

Doing her thing that no one understands, Christmas was telling signor Alberto that Annie wanted to know about his family when, all of a sudden, my hiding memory clicked into my consciousness.

"Geppetto! That's who he looks like, a younger Geppetto!"

Signor Alberto had evidently been told this many times before because he grinned from ear to ear and nodded in affirmation, his Geraldo-type mustache wiggling merrily.

"Aww . . . ." Suzanne loved any story as much as I did and was glad to find Pinocchio's kind papa right there in front of her.

Once, Suzanne and I threw a Mad Hatter's Tea Party, and it was a great success. I wondered if we could talk anyone into dressing up like Pinocchio. The cat was right there on the couch with Diana, and I was sure a few Jiminy Crickets were out and about. Before I could bring up the idea, signor Alberto rose from his chair. It was fairly evident that he was saying it was time for him to leave and that he had enjoyed his visit very much. Christmas's gift seemed to be rubbing off on me and for that, I was glad.

Just before he put one foot outside, I caught the quick look Alberto shot at Christmas who was holding the door. I punched Jules in the ribs and motioned for her to see what I saw. Because the look had already passed, she didn't see it and nagged me all the way back to the couch to tell her what I was signaling about.

I plopped down beside her and whispered, "Looks as if we may have another romance budding under our noses."

"No way!" Jules tried to whisper back although she was too shocked to keep her voice down.

"You just wait," I said.

I'm one of those people who can do most anything—except algebra and things I don't want to do like scuba diving. However, I don't excel at anything, not that I can remember, anyway. But I do have the God-given gift of seeing into the hearts of people, and that day I saw something akin to adoration bubbling over in signor Alberto's heart. Christmas, on the other hand, was not there as yet although she obviously liked him very much. But Christmas likes everyone which I think I've said before.

Annie saw it, too. I could tell. I watched her smile slightly and file the thought away for later. *Time will tell* is very near the top in her philosophy of life.

Although Diana tried hard not to show it, she was getting impatient for Mario to arrive. He had planned to be back by dinner, but dinner was over and we had enjoyed a nice visit with the neighbor. He was late. Any other time, none of us would have been concerned about one hour. Goodness gracious, we never knew when Jules would show up for anything. But the rather precarious events that had taken place during this journey caused us to acquire a different attitude towards being late. What if d'Corsa and his sidekick had other accomplices? What if they were part of a gang? Are there gangs in Italy? *Of course, there are gangs,* I told myself. *The Mafia was born here.*

In consideration of Lyn and her inclination to worry, I kept my thoughts to myself throughout the next half hour or so and then excused myself to go to my room. Some of the others were drifting off as well. I paused on the landing to look back. Diana lounged with her feet on an ottoman trying to keep her mind on the book she had been reading. Over on the sofa, Christmas was softly strumming her guitar. Annie was reading near the huge fireplace. It was a charming, peaceful scene, but I knew my friends were worried about Mario, particularly Diana. I was, too.

Quite unusual for me, sleep must have overcome me as soon as my head hit my goose down pillow. My last thought was to wonder if I was lying on the down from one of our little goslings' cousins. Then I thought, *who on earth is in this house?* I heard voices and lots of them, male voices and more than just Mario's. No one sounded particularly upset, so my normal reaction would have been to turn over and go back to sleep. Nevertheless, curiosity got the best of me, and I slipped on my robe and scurried down the stairs as fast as my stiff joints would allow.

"Signora Marnie, I am so happy you came down." Mario arose and took my hand.

"Mario, you are a sight for sore eyes. We were so worried about you."

The quizzical look on our new friend's face told me he was not familiar with that particular Southern expression, but it wasn't the time to explain. He let it go as well and turned to introduce me to the two men who had stood up with him when I came in.

"This is the friend I have spoken of quite often, Inspector Franco, from Firenze."

The gallant Italian took my hand and softly kissed it which I had assumed was a French thing. Obviously, I was wrong. "Welcome to Italy, signora."

Surprisingly, he spoke very good English with only a slight accent, much better than Mario, actually. He was rather short, slim and reminded me somewhat of Inspector Clouseau, the Peter Sellers character in the Pink Panther films, remember him? He once said, "The crooks never sleep and neither does Clouseau!" Neither did Inspector Franco, it seemed.

The other, taller man was your average Italian hunk, much younger than anyone else in the room. He was very polite and rather humble, I must say.

The other sleepers drifted into the room one-by-one, receiving the same gracious welcome from Mario and starting introductions all over again. It must have been a half hour after I awoke when we finally got down to business.

Inspector Franco began. "Mario has told me all about you, signoras." He had an interesting one-sided smile.

"Oh, dear," said Christmas.

We laughed lightheartedly and from that moment on, it seemed we had all been friends forever. Inspector Franco turned out to be a very humorous man for one in his profession, and his sidekick, Giovanni, remained quiet as a mouse. He sat beside Annie on a sofa which seemed perfectly natural because our Annie is always adopting young men as their counselor and mentor. I can't tell you the number of young guys who have gone on to make something of their lives because of Annie's influence. I was sure this relationship was headed in a similar direction.

"I apologize for visiting so late at night, but I find it urgent to ask you a few questions in person." His smile was a bit quirky considering its one-sidedness, but it was certainly genuine.

"To prepare for the lineup, right?" Like me, Jules wanted to make sure she understood.

"Ahh . . . ." The inspector glanced at Mario, and I knew instantly that something was off kilter.

"The lineup may have to be postponed a day or two," said Franco, rather cautiously, I thought.

Lyn just closed her eyes.

I thought it rather odd that he gave no more explanation than that, but I decided to leave it alone for the time being. I could ask questions later.

He turned to me. "Signora Marnie?"

"Yes."

"You were the first to see this man you thought was Lucien d'Corsa, yes?"

"Yes. I met him in the airport rest . . . , ah . . . in the Rome airport. And I must say he was not a very friendly man."

"You spoke with him?"

"Yes, because I thought he was the artist, you see."

"Yes, yes, I understand."

He then turned in Lyn's direction. "And signora Lyn, you were the next to see him?"

Her reply was almost a whisper. "Yes, I saw him but not very clearly. Mostly, I saw the back of his head as he went down the corridor. The only time I saw his face was when he came out of the rest—" her eyes flickered towards me, "the restroom. It was just a quick glance. I'm really not sure I would recognize him."

"But you saw him other places as well? Roma? Venezia? The village market nearby, yes?"

For a few seconds it was questionable whether or not Lyn would answer, but finally she whispered, "Yes, but . . . but he made me so nervous that I'm not sure I ever really looked into his face."

"I understand perfectly, signora."

Suzanne was next. "And you saw this man in Venice. Is that correct?"

"Yes. I think he chased Marnie and me in a gondola."

"Chased you?" Mario chuckled. "In a gondola?"

"Well," I inserted, "he followed us. Wouldn't that be more correct, Suze?"

"I guess so, but I felt like I was being chased."

I nodded because I had felt the same way.

"My problem is that he always wore that red beret. I'm really not sure if I would recognize him without it." Suzanne frowned in thought.

That set all our heads nodding in agreement.

Suzanne continued. "Inspector, don't you think it's strange that this man would wear something that made him look like a woodpecker at a penguin convention?"

It took a while for that to sink in, but when it did, the inspector guffawed from the bottom of his little belly. "I agree, signora, it is very strange." He continued to chuckle causing Christmas and Mario to join in.

"It's almost as if he wanted us to know he was following us," said Diana. She is very talented at turning a meeting back on focus.

"Hmm," mused the inspector. "Very strange indeed.... And you are sure, signora Marnie, that the man who broke into this villa was the same man?"

"No, not really. I only guessed it was him by Angelica's description of the burglar. I never saw the man that night."

"And you, signora Jules, did you see him?"

"No, sorry. I had to keep my eyes on the road. And it was all I could do to avoid hitting the sheep."

The inspector stared at Jules as did Giovanni. I'm not sure but I think I sensed a bit of admiration in his eyes.

"So, bottom line is, as you say in the States, no one is positive the man who broke in the villa is the same man who followed you. Correct?"

Again, we nodded in symphony, agreeing unanimously.

"Very interesting."

I jumped in to explain my answers a little better. "Nevertheless, the man at the market *was* the same man, right Suzanne? Right, Lyn?"

Lyn nodded again as Suzanne replied, "Right. He was one and the same."

"I understand." The inspector smiled at Suzanne. More than likely, he was still picturing the woodpecker and the penguins.

My admiration for the inspector was growing. He didn't take one note. Evidently, his memory was excellent, and if there is something I admire these days, it's a good memory considering the state of my own.

"Thank you very much, signoras." Inspector Franco stood to say his goodbyes. "Officer Giovanni and I will be driving back to Firenze where I will record my report. I will let Mario know of further developments. You have been most gracious." He gave a slight bow and turned to leave.

"Wait, Inspector." Annie got up and walked over to Franco. "You said the lineup has been postponed. Why is that?"

"I was hoping you would not ask me that question, signora. However, I am sorry to say that the head of our . . . ah, precinct, does not believe we have enough evidence on this man to keep him in jail. He was released just before Mario and I left Firenze to come here."

Out of the corner of my eye I saw Lyn's hands fly up to cover her face. Suzanne gasped.

Jules looked overcome. "But we know he was the one on the highway that night. Mario got his license number."

"Si, and he may have to go to court for unsafe driving, but we cannot prove he did anything other than that. My captain said that because you were chasing the truck, the judge may not convict him of unsafe driving. You admitted yourself that you chased him and also that you passed him and tried to stop him on the highway. Is that not correct?"

"Yeah." Jules looked deflated, staring into thin air.

Annie asked everyone's question. "What happens now?"

"We wait to see what he will do next if anything. I am sorry."

Lyn told me later that she was literally sick to her stomach when Inspector Franco said that. It was just more than she could take to know that our stalker was out there somewhere and could break in on us again any minute of the day or night.

The inspector seemed to read her thoughts. "Mario has agreed to take time off from his work to stay with you the remainder of your holiday in Italy. He will call me if there is any hint of wrongdoing. I am sure you will be safe."

Diana glanced sidelong at Mario and smiled. Her knight in shining armor—the armor a nice black T-shirt with black pants and sandals—beamed a broader smile back at her and inched a little closer.

"I want to go home." Lyn sounded as if her life depended upon it, and it may have.

"We canceled the flight, remember?" Diana stepped back to where Lyn was still sitting and placed her hand on Lyn's shoulder.

I knew my mouth looked like that frown symbol on the computer, :o(. It's a thing I inherited from my grandmother, and I hate it but that's just the way it is. I've practiced a pleasant expression for years in front of many mirrors, but alas, my mouth prefers to frown.

Annie spoke to the inspector again. "We'll work all this out, Inspector. Don't worry. We understand your position."

"*Grazie,* signora," he replied. Nodding a few more times, Inspector Franco walked out the door followed by Giovanni. Then he stopped short, and Giovanni bumped into his back.

"Mario," he said, turning around, "why do I not leave Giovanni with you and the signoras? It would not hurt to have another man around."

Jules popped out of her reverie. "We'll be fine, Inspector. I'm sure we can take care of ourselves. I've done it for many years."

"I am sure you can, signora Jules, but sometimes it is safer this way. Giovanni has been trained in karate; black belt I think, right Giovanni?" The inspector chuckled, glancing at Giovanni who looked as pliant as silly putty. "He does not seem very aggressive, but I assure you, if the need arose, Giovanni could fight off an army."

While Giovanni blushed and we all smiled, the inspector walked out the door once again. Mario walked him to his car.

Suzanne, the sister with a servant's heart, is also the practical one when it comes to everyday living. "Do you have clothing, Giovanni? And what about other things you'll need like a toothbrush? Giovanni, do you speak English?"

"Si, signora. But no, I do not have anything with me. I was not expecting this assignment."

"Join the club," whispered Jules.

Suzanne didn't hear her. "Don't worry. We have extra everything. Marnie has enough Sensodyne toothpaste for every tooth in Italy."

At that, Giovanni laughed, the first time he had expressed any emotion since he arrived.

"You can take my room, and I'll move in with Jules. She has two beds."

Suzanne was already moving towards the stairs to collect everything Giovanni would need.

Diana hurried over to catch Suzanne as fast as etiquette would allow, and I joined them to find out what was going on.

Quietly, Diana said, "Why don't we put Giovanni downstairs with Mario? Don't you think that would be better?"

"You mean more proper?" I was a bit concerned about that as well.

"Yes." Diana's expression was sober.

"No," replied Suzanne, "He should be upstairs with us. We'll have a man downstairs and one upstairs. And I don't know about Mario, but Giovanni has a gun. I saw it under his jacket."

"I see," said Diana.

"Anyway, he's too young for any of us, so there shouldn't be a problem in that area."

"You're right about that," replied Diana.

"Not necessarily," I said. "Remember that movie we saw not long ago? The British lady went on holiday and had an affair with that young guy in Barcelona."

"Marn, that only happens in movies. This is real life. Plus, it's not in our moral makeup to do such a thing."

"True, but we don't know Giovanni very well."

"Marn, look at the guy. He can't be more than twenty-five. Now look around you. See anyone you think might interest him?"

As usual, Suzanne was right, so right that Diana walked off in the middle of the conversation to join Mario on the sofa.

"Come on," I said, leading Suzanne up the stairs. "I'll get the toothpaste."

Chapter Fifteen

"WOULD YOU LOOK AT THAT?" Jules and I were taking a walk down the stone path that wound its way through the perennial garden and down to the pool.

I looked up from the purple delphiniums I had been admiring. "I told you so."

There sat Christmas and Alberto, sipping lemonade and feeding the little goslings crumbs from the scones they were nibbling on. They were so engrossed in their own little world that neither of them noticed that Jules and I were close at hand until Jules spoke.

"Hey. What's going on?"

"Jules!" Christmas smiled, visibly surprised by our presence. "Hi, Marnie."

"You two look as if you're having a nice time." I spoke in a little bit of a teasing tone.

"You sure do," said Jules, grinning.

"We are," said Christmas. "It's nice out here."

As Alberto smiled at us, his mustache wiggled happily. His greeting was just as cheery. *"Boun giorno, Boun giorno!"*

"Boun giorno, signor Alberto," said Jules.

"Pull up a chair and join us," Christmas said.

"We're going to walk a while," I said. "I need more exercise than usual with Angelica in the kitchen."

"I know," replied Christmas. "Me, too. Want to go swimming later, Jules?"

"Yes. I was hoping you'd ask. I've wanted to jump in all day. Want to go a few laps now? I have my suit on under my shorts just in case."

Christmas sat there a few seconds smiling at Jules and then turned to glance at Alberto. "Um ... no, I think I'll wait until later, maybe after dinner."

"I know," said I, "let's have dinner outside tonight, down here by the pool under that lovely rose trellis. Wouldn't that be nice? We'll put a white tablecloth on the table, and perhaps Diana will create one of her beautiful flower arrangements for the centerpiece. Oh, I'm so excited! I've seen this scene played out in so many movies and travel magazines, and now I'm going to really live it, not just vicariously." My mind was going a mile a minute with plans for our candlelight evening in the garden by the pool. "Jules, you do this all the time on your property at home. Come on. We can plan while we walk."

My eye caught a glimpse of Christmas as we started off. She looked a little sheepish, one might say. I held up my hand for Jules to wait. "What is it, Christmas?"

I think she blushed, but the sun was pretty bright so I'm not sure. "What about signor Alberto?"

"I'm so glad you said that. Invite him, of course. The more, the merrier."

Jules and I waved goodbye and began our trek again.

"Have you thought how different tonight will be?"

"You mean having dinner outside by the pool?"

"Not that," I said. "For the first time, we will have three men at the table. Won't that be nice?"

"Uh, huh, but Marnie, think about it. Alberto can't speak a word of English, and Giovanni doesn't seem to talk period. That leaves us right back where we started in Rome with Mario." Jules laughed, and I had to join her.

"Well, who knows? Someone else might show up. It certainly wouldn't surprise me."

And that's exactly what happened. Inspector Clouseau, alias Franco, came back just in time for dinner. I wondered if he had a wife to cook for him, but I hated to ask. Perhaps the dinner conversation could be steered in that direction at some point.

Except for Angelica's concern for all that walking back and forth from the kitchen to the pool, the preparations went wonderfully. After Suzanne assured our emotional cook that the serving cart could roll down to the garden just as easily as into the living room, she seemed better. Furthermore, there were seven of us as well as Pisa and Mario to help. We sisters took complete charge of the table area with Mario, Giovanni and Alberto as our gophers.

Jules, who adores candles and has them stationed everywhere in her house at home, went on a candle hunt throughout the entire villa, ending up with about seventy-five to one-hundred candles in her basket. While each of us fulfilled our assigned task, Jules happily placed candles everywhere from the table to the flower beds and all around the pool. She even talked Mario and Giovanni into lugging two wrought iron standing candelabras down to our outdoor dining room. Signor Alberto let Christmas know that he wanted to help more, so Jules recruited him to help her light all the candles when it was time.

I'm telling you, when I walked down that path with Lyn after dressing in my finest attire, I was translated into another world. Lyn gasped so deeply it's a wonder she didn't choke. And in that moment, she did a three-hundred-and-sixty-degree turnabout. It was as if she walked through some type of force field that took with it all her worries and fears. She floated throughout that fairy-tale night with a sweet, contented smile on her face. I watched each of our sisters as they stared at Lyn with big smiles and then greeted her as if this was the first time they had seen her during the entire trip.

She even chatted during dinner, and I'm sure it wasn't the wine because Lyn never drinks more than a sip or two if that. Signor Alberto, using the few English words Christmas had taught him and a whole lot of hand expressions, managed to tell us a little about his extensive vegetable garden. Being a farmer herself, Lyn took great interest in trying to figure out what he was saying, even adding her own expertise in growing tomatoes at one point. She seemed to have developed that telepathic thing from Christmas because, by the time the evening was over, Senior Alberto had invited her to see his garden and possibly give him a few tips. She also seemed to have developed a wonderful rapport with Alberto, probably because they both have farmer's hearts. Christmas was thrilled that Alberto had another friend. I was thrilled that Lyn had one.

Giovanni was another story. Shy and introverted, he sat by Annie and just smiled. I did notice that the two of them carried on a few short conversations between themselves, and I was happy that he, too, had made a friend. And knowing Annie as I did, I was sure the friendship would last a lifetime. I tried my best to picture Giovanni in a karate fight beating up the bad guys, but I just could not pull it up in my mind's eye. Finally, I let it go and dismissed the fleeting thought that I might see him fight in actuality if our own personal bad guy showed up again.

That night our enchanted garden crossed into another dimension. My one concern was that Inspector Franco would want to talk about the case, but he didn't. Or if he did, he changed his mind. Probably, the latter. Around midnight, I glanced at each of my friends and knew that not one of them wanted to leave. Soft Italian love songs from Jules's iPod, twinkling lights and flickering candles, fluffs of green hydrangeas and white Queen Anne's Lace—our surroundings comforted our souls and lifted all worries and cares from our minds. I think we all were afraid that leaving our garden would be like the children stepping back through the wardrobe from the magic of Narnia.

As we sipped coffee poured from a lovely antique silver urn, I saw Alberto slip out of his seat and reach for something lying on a lounge chair. As he tucked an old violin under his chin and reached for the bow, Jules crept over to turn off the iPod. The sweet, sweet strains that came from that old violin seeped into our souls, healing and cleansing whatever was still there of our worries and fears. Tears poured down Lyn's cheeks but this time, they were tears of joy and peace. And she wasn't the only one who wept while the music soothed our souls.

As quiet as a mouse, Mario slipped from his chair and offered Diana his hand. Beaming her most beautiful smile, she accepted it as graciously as a queen. He led her to the stone patio beside the table. They began to dance, slowly at first, just simple steps over the smooth stone. And then the music transitioned into a beautiful waltz tune from romantic days gone by. Mario and Diana smiled into one another's eyes and began to move with the music like flowing water in a clear stream. Around and around the patio they swirled, Diana's pale blue dress soft and willowy and dreamy. On and on they danced while the Tuscan moon peeped at us through the arbor vines that hung low with sweet-smelling grapes. It was a perfect end to a perfect evening. Like Annie said that night on the Grand Canal in Venice, I thought, *this is what heaven will be.*

Chapter Sixteen

THE FOLLOWING MORNING, I waited as long as I could stand it and then called Pete to catch him up on our infamous adventures as well as to tell him about our fantastic evening by the pool and how much I missed him.

Like most husbands still in love with their wives after forty-something years, his first words were, "Why in tarnation are you staying over there with that lunatic following you around? I want you to come home."

"Oh, we're fine, sugar. We even have police protection. This young guy is a black belt who looks like he wouldn't harm a fly if it pitched on his nose. What's more, Inspector Franco comes in and out—more in than out these days. He says his reason is to talk about the case with Mario, but I know better. Pete, the man is hungry, and our Angelica is the best cook in Tuscany. Oh, and we have signor Alberto, too."

"Who's he?" Pete didn't sound too convinced of our safety.

"He's the farmer next door, and Pete, he looks just like Geppetto in Pinocchio."

"Who?"

"Oh, I forgot you never read fairy tales. He's . . . ."

"Forget it, Marn. You can show me the pictures when you get back. I'm glad you have protection, but don't take any chances. Did you get that pistol I told you to buy?"

"No, but I did get some mace or something like that. I promise you I'll spray the first crook that comes near me."

"You may not know it's a crook."

"That's true, but don't worry, sugar. I'll be home before long."

"Well . . . okay. I miss you."

"I miss you, too. Hug all the grandchildren for me."

It was hard to fight the melancholy that tried to overtake me as we said goodbye. I have loved that man since he was sixteen years old and weighed all of 145 pounds soaking wet. I sure did miss him.

My pensive mood had almost lifted when Diana and Suzanne came in. Diana took a seat in the Louis the Fourteenth chair, and Suzanne flopped on the bed. While my mouth opened to greet them, Annie and Jules meandered in.

"Christmas took Lyn over to see signor Alberto's garden," said Diana. "Wasn't it awesome to see the change in her last night?"

"I could hardly believe my eyes," replied Suzanne.

Jules smiled. "I just hope it sticks."

"It will," I responded with a smile. "Our Lyn has experienced what one might call a *breakthrough*."

"That's the truth." Suzanne plumped the pillows to make herself more comfortable. She started plaiting Jules long tresses which made them look like little girls at a sleepover, especially with Annie lying across the end of the bed at their feet.

I admired Jules's long hair. "You hair is still so thick and healthy."

"And yours isn't?" Jules grinned at me. "Your hair looks nice, Marn."

"It's getting very thin compared to what it used to be, especially on the crown of my head."

"Mine, too," said Annie. "I don't know what happened to my hair." She patted her head as if she might find the missing hair.

"Well, I know where mine is. About a quarter of the hair on my head slowly migrated to various other parts of my body over the past few years. Not too long ago, there was a strong magnifying mirror in a hotel I was staying in, and I discovered the migratory pattern. See this?" I paused to point at my chin. "Right there on the cusp of my bottom lip. I guess I'd have a goatee if Lyn didn't wax it now and then."

They all laughed, and Jules even felt her lip to see if it had happened to her. "Don't worry, Jules," I said, "you're still too young."

"Did you find any more?" Annie was literally giggling, something she didn't often do.

"I sure did. While I was looking in the mirror, staring at my little white goatee, a clump of hair jumped out my nose and attached itself to the rim of my nostrils. Can't wax that. I have to shave it."

You just can't beat female camaraderie. We laughed until we cried. Diana almost broke the Louis the Fourteenth chair trying to get out of it to look in the mirror to check her chin and nose.

"You can't see it in *that* mirror," I said. "You need at least a sixteen times strength mirror."

"That might be why I didn't think I had that problem," said Annie. "It's there; I just can't see it."

The laughter started all over again while Diana examined her face the best she could in the weak mirror on the wall.

"You know," said Diana, "when I was young, I couldn't bear the thought of becoming one of those women who miss their lips when they put their lipstick on and sometimes wear purple eye shadow, probably because they think its soft grey. I do hope that doesn't happen to me."

"Don't worry," I replied. "We'll help you with your makeup if you end up in that condition."

"You! You're five years older than I am! You're not helping me with *my* makeup, Marn."

"I can probably see your face better than mine. Or, I could use a magnifying glass."

"Forget it." The others were still laughing, but I could tell Diana was a bit concerned.

"You know, Lyn sometimes puts makeup on corpses when she does their hair. Want her to do yours?"

I thought it was a reasonable inquiry, but Diana's eyes suddenly looked as round as the moon. "She's older than *you!*"

"True, but she's trained."

"Annie," said Diana rather soberly, "do not let these girls make me up, dead or alive. Promise?"

"I promise, but I'm the oldest. I'll probably be dead by then myself." I don't know when I've seen Annie enjoy herself so much.

Christmas peeped around the door frame. "Let's have a picnic for lunch today."

"Sounds great," said Jules.

We all agreed it was a wonderful idea.

"Where shall we go?" Diana took one more look in the mirror and turned to await a reply from Christmas.

Lyn came into the room, huffing a little from the stairs and the very long trek to Alberto's garden.

"There is a beautiful pond on Alberto's land. He invited us to have a picnic there anytime."

Lyn took a deep breath and said, "You mean I've got to walk all the way back?"

Christmas threw her arm around Lyn's shoulders. "No, no, don't worry. Alberto said for us to ask Mario about the golf carts in the garage. The owner keeps them for this type of excursion."

Lyn let out her breath.

"That would be fun," said Jules. "I can drive a golf cart."

I grinned. "Better than a motorcycle, I hope."

"Funny, Marn."

Suzanne hopped off the bed. "Let's go see what we can find to eat. Surely, there are lots of leftovers from last night. Come help me, Lyn."

Annie got up to help as well while I waited for my assignment.

Christmas said, "Why don't you go ask Mario about the golf carts, Diana? I'll join you in a few minutes. Need to wash up."

"Sure. Come with me, Marnie. Can you drive a golf cart? We'll need more than one, maybe three, for all of us."

"I can drive anything without a clutch, and I can use a clutch, but sometimes they prove to be problematic for me."

From the look on Diana's face, I could tell my assignment would not be driving a golf cart. We rode around in something like that at the beach once with Diana steering, but we had to pedal with our feet. We looked like seven Wilma Flintstones in a stone age Mercedes.

Mario greeted Diana and me as we descended the stairs. "Guess who is here?"

"Inspector Franco, what a surprise." Diana held out her hand.

"You lie," I whispered from behind.

"The inspector has a few more questions for you and also a new report to give."

The inspector was kissing my hand which I will have to say is a most delightful custom. "I hope you have good news, Inspector."

Diana asked, "I think in this case any news is good news, don't you?"

"You're right about that. But first things first," I said. "Mario, have you invited Inspector Franco to join our picnic?"

"I did, and he graciously accepted the invitation."

The man must be starving, I thought. For the first time, I noticed how thin he was.

"How nice," Diana smiled at the inspector and then turned to Mario. "Mario, signor Alberto said you would know about the golf carts in the garage. Could we use them this afternoon? Christmas says Alberto's pond is too far away to walk."

"Of course," replied Mario, smiling down at her as if she had asked for a kiss. Inspector Franco will help me get them ready, right, Inspector?"

"Si, I will be glad to help."

"We have another option, *Cherie amour.*" Mario gazed into Diana's eyes as if he were offering her the world.

This time she must have blushed from head to toe, it being the first time Mario had used such an endearing term in public. I'm sure that night she got down on her knees and thanked God her public consisted of only the inspector who paid it no mind and me who did.

"The stables are only a half mile from the house, and the horses are available for the guests. Do you think that any of the signoras would like to ride to the picnic?"

Diana's face lit up. "What a wonderful idea. I would like to, and I'm positive that Jules will ride. I don't know about the others, but I will ask. What about you, Marnie?"

"Well, my heart would love it, but my repertoire of talents does not include riding horses. I'll stick with the golf cart even if it has a clutch."

Bless her heart, Diana was so excited she forgot her embarrassment and hurried to ask if the other sisters wanted to ride horses to the picnic.

In the end, Diana, Jules, Christmas, Suzanne and Mario mounted up, and the rest of us followed in the golf carts driven by Inspector Franco and Annie. I sat back and enjoyed the new vistas along the way.

The path led us through signor Alberto's vineyards as well as his olive grove which led me to wonder if *farmer* was the best description for his occupation. I tried to think of all the words that might describe him, husbandman being one. I've always thought that odd. It sounds as if a man is married to a grapevine. Having no idea what an olive grower is called other than an olive grower, my word game didn't last long.

Following the extremely extensive olive grove was an even more extensive sheep pasture, possibly the same pasture Jules and I landed in the night of the burglary. Having a great fondness for sheep—why, I don't know—I watched the animals with great interest. The woolly creatures are quite beautiful from afar, but up close, they seem to be rather dirty and look as if they have rolled in hay all day. I can only assume that's the reason Jesus used them in illustrations so often, comparing us with the dirty, stubborn, dumb little creatures. Perhaps it's also the reason I like them so much. It's an identification thing.

Pond was another misnomer we had used in speaking of signor Alberto's property. The thing was a lake if I've ever seen one. In fact, we could hardly see to the other side and little waves lapped up on a narrow sandy shore. Like everywhere we had been in Tuscany, the place was absolutely beautiful. Alberto met us there in a lovely area he had chosen for our picnic consisting of pleasant shade trees and freshly mown grass. Lavender wildflowers wandered off in the distance meeting with the blue horizon far away.

The riders tied their horses to trees far enough away that we wouldn't get a whiff of any smelly activities. The horses seemed perfectly content to munch on the sweet grass and rest which would certainly have been my idea of a picnic if I were a horse.

Angelica had helped Suzanne, Lyn and Annie pack our lunch, and never in my life had I seen so much food on the ground. I take that back. When I was a little girl, I attended a country church with my grandfather. Once a year, the church celebrated its existence by inviting all its previous and present members to come back for a lot of preaching, a lot of singing and a lot of food on the church grounds. The event was naturally called *homecoming*. Actually, the food wasn't really *on the ground* but spread out on a long chicken wire banquet table tied between two trees. Those were the best banana sandwiches I've ever eaten in my life. And what's more, the sandwiches, the potato salad and the deviled eggs stayed in the sun all afternoon and didn't even kill us.

Upon request, Alberto brought his violin, and this time, he played lively tunes to which he quite often danced while he played. It was a marvelous sight to see. We all clapped for a while, but finally, we couldn't help but join him. Not a one of us had a clue as to how to dance in Italian, but we made the best of it with Mario and Inspector Franco leading the way. The inspector turned out to be much more socially-minded than I first thought. Until that day, police business and food had seemed his only interests. However, it was during our delightful Italian folk dancing that I first noticed his attention had taken a new direction. Annie, who had danced about as much as I had in her life, twirled and whirled with the best of them, a breakthrough I have to attribute to Inspector Franco.

"Goodness gracious," I murmured. One affair was flowering; one was budding, and one was just past budding. Unlike Diana, I couldn't imagine Annie living in Italy. She was too homebound with so many grandchildren. The inspector would have to move to the States. I just hoped there wasn't a wife behind the scenes. Certainly, Mario would have told us, but then I thought, *He is Italian.*

As I watched the dancing, I realized I was getting carried away, but I just couldn't help it. And then I stopped my musing because Mario, like Calgon, carried me away.

That evening, we were seven exhausted women. Other than Jules, those who traveled on horseback had ridden only occasionally in the past few years, and they were naturally much more exhausted than those of us who rode the golf cart. Although tired, Suzanne, who had asked for a mild-mannered mount, came back wired for more of the same. I had a feeling

Jules would be giving riding lessons soon.

Angelica was given the night off, a gift to which she responded by pouting all the next day. Apparently, she preferred to stay with us. We were all too tired to eat or do much of anything else. In fact, a few of us groaned when Mario sent word to our rooms by Pisa that Inspector Franco wanted to have a meeting.

"Not tonight," grumbled Suzanne, rubbing her hind parts.

Lyn just shook her head in obvious agreement. "All that dancing last night and today added to the long walk to see Alberto's garden has worn me out."

"Pisa," said Diana, "please ask Mario to ask the inspector if we can be excused. We can't make it, and that's that."

Pisa by this time had somehow developed that same telepathic thing as Christmas and then Lyn. I wondered if this way of communicating would be prevalent in heaven.

In a few short moments, Pisa was back to get Diana. Mario had evidently asked for her. Within another few short moments, Diana was back, and although she said nothing, it was obvious we wouldn't have a meeting that night. Christmas and I exchanged smiles.

Chapter Seventeen

INSPECTOR FRANCO FINALLY GOT HIS MEETING. I think he must have stayed the night again. Why he wasn't needed in Florence, I don't know. Perhaps our case was top priority. It was certainly mine.

Owing to my lifelong habit of promptness, I walked into the living room about ten minutes early to find a most interesting sight. The inspector and Annie stood together by the wide glass-paned doors opening to the courtyard as quiet as two stone lions guarding the gate. Thankfully, they were unaware of my arrival because in a few moments they continued what I guessed to be a previous conversation. Unfortunately, I was too far away to hear what they said, but it seemed to be a very pleasant chat although our Annie isn't known to chat very often. If anything is important enough to speak aloud, she speaks, but if it isn't, she usually leaves it unsaid.

Although I couldn't hear their voices, my view of the couple was clear, so in the moments before my other sisters entered the room, I watched closely and tried to read their body language. I found that task rather difficult because, unlike Diana and Mario, the two were hard to read. In the end, I gave up, but only for the time being.

"Buon giorno, everyone!" Diana flowed into the room like Loretta Young, remember her? I always loved the way she entered a room, her dress carried by the wind she created in her movement. In she would come with a broad smile on her beautiful face.

The greetings continued for quite a while owing to Diana's setting the jovial mood. It seemed we were all in high spirits that day. However, the inspector's news brought us down a notch or two. After making ourselves comfortable in our favorite sofas and chairs, Inspector Franco gave us his report.

"I miei amici," he began, "the investigation has uncovered a fact you may not have anticipated."

I could actually feel our ears prick. Each of us gazed at the inspector with what Dickens called, "Great Expectations."

"The man that signora Marnie thought to be the great artist, Lucien d'Corsa, is actually a member of a widely connected crime syndicate."

"Oh, my goodness," gasped Lyn.

"The *Mafia?*" Jules looked wild-eyed.

"No, no, not the old Mafia you hear about on American television." The inspector obviously thought his reply would comfort us, but whether the Mafia was new or old was of no concern to us. The Mafia is the Mafia.

The inspector continued. "The man's name is Carlos Panzinni. Have any of your ever heard that name?"

"No, I haven't," I replied as the others shook their heads.

"And you, Mario, have you heard this name?"

"Hmm, no, I do not think I have."

"My sources say that this man is what you might call in America, the mole for the burglary operation of the syndicate. Although the officials in Roma hear about this type of crime much more than we do because they host the principal airport in Italy, my office has dealt with this before. I had my suspicions, but I wanted to wait for proof before I spoke."

Suzanne asked the question on the tip of my tongue. "Other than the infuriating little creatures that ruin my lawn, what is a mole?"

"The spy or perhaps the scout. In this case, the person who was sent out to find vulnerable targets for the operation."

"Like us." Christmas said it, but we all thought it.

"Si, women like you are the most vulnerable. You dress nicely. You wear jewelry. You can obviously afford nice places to stay. And most of all, you have no man to protect you."

I couldn't help but speak up at that, and Jules was right on my trail. "I honestly do not understand how a man could keep a burglar away any better than a woman."

"Me, either," quipped Jules. She looked almost angry.

All I could think about was Annie and how she was going to have to teach this man a thing or two if they were going to have a relationship of any kind. He was living in the Dark Ages.

"Ah, signora, Italians believe that the man is the protector of women. We put our women on pedestals. Is this not so in America?"

"Not necessarily," replied Jules. "I have raised four children and taken care of seven acres without a man for more years than I care to remember."

Diana added, "I've never been married, Inspector. And I've never been robbed, either."

"Butch is a big ex-football player, but when he's not around, I don't quiver in my boots," said Suzanne rather testily.

Mario was having a ball. Grinning from ear to ear, he looked from one of us to the other awaiting what would be said next. The inspector wasn't so pleased with the way the meeting was going. Finally, he looked over at Annie, his eyes imploring her help.

"Don't look at me," she said. "I've always taken care of myself, and I've done a pretty good job. I've never been robbed or attacked or anything else."

"Well," said I, "Pete is a wonderful protector, but half the time he doesn't even know where I am and vice versa. Christmas has traveled the world completely on her own, and although Lyn has Pops, she can shoot a gun with the best. That Panzinni man has no idea who he's tangling with, I can tell you that."

"Don't forget the angels, Marnie," said Christmas with a smile.

"Angels?" Inspector Franco's voice almost failed him. The man looked totally defeated.

"Yes," I replied. "We believe there are guardian angels all around us, as a group and personally as well. Christmas has seen hers."

The others nodded in agreement as Mario's handsome eyebrows went up and the inspector's spirit went down. The remainder of the day, I could tell he avoided Christmas. Apparently, he didn't want to hear about her angel.

Inspector Franco clasped his hands between his boney knees and looked down as if trying to figure out how to unclasp them. If Mario hadn't rescued him, I think the man might have stayed in that position forever. We could have poured cement over him and made a statue like *The Thinker*.

"Signoras, I believe you have made your point." Mario tried to stifle a laugh, but he couldn't. "From now on, I promise that neither the inspector nor I will refer to you in any way as vulnerable or helpless women."

"Thank you very much," said Diana, throwing him a teasing smile.

"So what happens now, Inspector?" I asked.

Gradually, he lifted his head. "We are looking for Panzinni, but our foremost objective is to bring down this entire syndicate. Perhaps you can help?"

The man looked like a puppy begging for a treat. I was about to say *certainly* when Mario spoke up, grinning again. "Since you are all so self-sufficient, I am sure you will be willing to help."

"Of course," said Diana beaming him another smile.

"Wait," said Lyn, "does this mean we have to stay in Italy even longer?"

"Hopefully not," replied the inspector. "Let me explain my plan." He moved to the edge of his seat and leaned an elbow on each knee. Clasping his hands again, he unveiled the plan.

"I would like for you to take a day trip. Have you been to Pistoia as yet? The cathedral there is most beautiful. Si, Mario?"

"Yes, you will enjoy Pistoia very much." He spoke to us all but his eyes searched for Diana's. Then he added, "Some people find Pistoia very romantic, especially the Palazzo."

All eyes were now on Diana who was getting much better at handling public embarrassment. She only turned a slight shade of pink.

Jules stood and stretched her taut body. "Sounds good to me. I've enjoyed every second of our time here, but I would like to see more of Italy before we go home."

"Me, too," said Christmas.

We must have all looked fairly agreeable because the inspector went on with the plan. "Try not to think about Panzinni while you visit the beautiful places in Pistoia. But I do ask that you keep your eyes open in case he follows you. A few of our officers will be shadowing you, including me."

"In other words," I said, "you want us sitting ducks to act perfectly natural."

"Si."

"We can do that, girls," said Suzanne.

"Sure, we can. I thought the guy was following us way back in Rome, but I've had a wonderful time."

Lyn cut in. "But you thought he was an artist then, not a gangster."

"True." I took a few moments to ponder that. "But by Venice we suspected foul play in the air, right Suzanne?"

"Yep. You don't get chased in a gondola every day."

"What about you, Mario? Will you be with us?" I detected a bit of hope in Diana's tone.

"No, I think not. Franco and I discussed it last night, and we think you would seem more vul . . . ah . . . ."

Diana's eyebrows rose this time. *"Vulnerable* perhaps?"

"In other words," I added, "your little ducks will be more open to monkey business with no drake around."

"Drake?" Mario looked confused.

"A male duck." Diana's face was void of her normal smile.

"Ah, yes." He nodded quickly and turned from her piercing eyes. "You will take the van as usual and drive into Pistoia by the main highway. The inspector has made of list of places you will want to visit. Please keep to the list so that we will know where you are at all times."

"Si," said the inspector, "my men as well as Mario and I will be stationed nearby throughout the day."

"A covert operation," I remarked.

"Si, you may not see us all day but we will be there, nonetheless. If we see any sign of Panzinni or others we know to be connected with him, we will make our move and arrest them. Ah, and one more thing. If any of you were to spy this man, I want you to give us a signal. Only if you are absolutely sure you see him, I want you to lift your right hand as high as you can and wave happily as if you've seen a friend in the crowd. Can you do that?"

Jules jumped up and did as he instructed. Our runner was getting antsy with all the sitting around. "How's that?"

"Perfect, signora Jules." Inspector Franco glanced around at each of us, eager to receive affirmation that we understood the plan. When he got to Lyn, she shyly raised her hand and said, "I'm left-handed. What if I forget and raise my left hand?"

"It really does not matter which hand, does it, Franco?" I could tell Mario was more phlegmatic than the inspector.

"Oh, no. Either hand is fine."

I hoped all went well the next day for the inspector's sake as well as ours. The poor man's vigor seemed to have diminished as the meeting went on. Now, he looked like the thin, hungry man who first arrived at the villa to question us. All the food Angelica had fed him, the candlelight dancing, the delightful picnic and Annie's attention just faded away with the sunset.

Chapter Eighteen

SLEEP DIDN'T COME EASILY THAT NIGHT. My mind raced with speculations as to how the morrow would pan out. My grandmother used to say that what is going to be is going to be, and although I normally take her words to heart, I have found this statement to be consistently problematic. I'd like to call her up in heaven and say, "Not necessarily, Grandma." I consider life to be a series of choices.

Around midnight, I wondered if I should take a pill, but considering we had decided to do breakfast at nine and leave at ten, I was concerned I might not wake up on time. Consequently, when my cell phone played some crazy rock tune at eight a.m., I was one tired woman. I'll have to admit that I strongly considered backing out of the day's events entirely, but since I was the one who had seen our gangster friend most often, I knew there was no way to wiggle out of it.

After a nice hot shower and a glass of iced Coke—a Southern thing and one of my greatest weaknesses—I felt much better if not top notch. The others were electrified with excitement, or perhaps it was fear. I'm not sure. Studying my sisters' countenances as we devoured Angelica's appetizing breakfast was quite interesting.

Lyn sat stone-faced, picking at her food and taking a little bite every now and then. Suzanne had turned into her alias, Chatty Patty. She talked about everything from Butch's tendency to hog the television for sports to her newly acquired knowledge regarding the actuality of UFOs. Inspector Franco and Mario were visibly amazed. Our Suzanne was usually such a quiet little mouse.

There was really very little opportunity to get a word in edgewise, but now and then, Christmas popped up with a soft insertion—not necessarily related—and Jules made a few comments from her knowledge as a science teacher. I, on the other hand, kept quiet and listened even though I am extremely interested in UFOs. My theory is that they are angels or demons which agreed with some of Suzanne's ideas, but I didn't have time to get into that then. If I had, we would have still been sitting there at dinner.

Inspector Franco glanced at his watch which interested me because it seemed most everybody used cell phones to tell time in Italy as well as America. I am terribly concerned about watch companies going bankrupt, but perhaps they are owned by some mega-mogul like Fannie Mae and don't really need the income from the sale of watches. Anyway, the inspector looked as if he had something to say which Mario noticed at the same time I did. I saw him give Diana a look that was easy to read. Our Italian hunk—a phrase Jules often used—hated to interrupt Suzanne, and he was signaling Diana to do it for him.

She got it. "Is everyone finished with breakfast? We really need to get on the road."

Suzanne hushed instantly, and we all left the table to quickly brush our teeth and freshen up for the venturesome day ahead. My tiredness slipped away and was quickly replaced by nervousness, an emotion I don't often feel and one I don't like one bit. I'm sure all my friends felt the same though possibly not as much as I since so much depended on my identifying the crook.

The drive to Pistoia was delightful. In fact, I believe it helped a great deal with our nerve problem. Luscious pastures and vineyards slipped by, the pastures dotted with the little white sheep I held so dear. The vineyards reminded me that Alberto had told us his grapes would be ready for picking in a few more days, and I was hoping not to miss the grand event. If Lyn's life depended upon it, we would have to leave, but I couldn't help but hope our involvement with a crime syndicate would keep us in Italy just a few more days.

We arrived in Pistoia in the midst of a mass of people seemingly larger than the town.

"Oh, my goodness," said Lyn.

"Wow," said Annie who was driving, "I wonder if Inspector Franco knew that Saturday was market day in Pistoia."

"This crowd will make it much more difficult to spot Panzinni, that's for sure." I found it even more difficult to remember his name was Panzinni and not d'Corsa as I had called him for almost two weeks.

"Looks like fun," said Suzanne. She loves outdoor markets, flea or otherwise.

Annie miraculously found a parking place, and in no time at all, we were elbowing our way through the mass of mostly Italian humanity in the market square. I must say that the Italian language is like music to my ears. It's odd that some languages sound so harsh and uninviting while others are plain and blah, but not Italian. Never have I felt so welcomed in my life. Had I been rich with a U-Haul, I might have bought everything offered me in the market that day. Suzanne had a ball, and as usual, she came back with only one thin bag with a watercolor of the market inside.

After granting us free rein for a while, Diana drew us into a huddle and pulled out the list Inspector Franco had made. "We can't stay in the market all day. San Zeno Cathedral is first on the list."

"Surely, a gangster wouldn't follow us in there," said Christmas.

Suzanne piped up, "I forgot all about the gangster!"

"Christmas, don't you ever watch gangster movies? Every gangster I know machine-guns a bunch of people, and then, on his way home, he goes to church to ask forgiveness."

Christmas looked thoughtful. "Oh," she said.

Diana placed the list back in her purse and, having referred to the map accompanying the list, she led the way. "If Panzinni is nearby, hopefully he'll stay outside while we tour the cathedral. It looked magnificent on the net."

The cathedral resides in the center of Pistoia which made it quick and easy to find. We stopped to take pictures of the exterior which I found extremely interesting. Painted in black and white horizontal stripes, it was unlike any church I had ever seen. Although the architecture was, as Diana had said, magnificent, I found myself thinking of a jailhouse because of all those stripes. Sometimes, I have to pray certain pictures out of my mind so that I can see the real thing.

My next issue, after entering the grand edifice, was that its two patron saints were Zeno and Jacopo. Jacob, I knew but Zeno—could have been a woman for all I knew—was totally unfamiliar to me. I made a mental note to look Zeno up when I got back to the villa. I could have studied the literature that was readily available but no one wanted to wait for me to do research.

I must say that the cathedral was absolutely beautiful. Black and white was used in the interior design as well, creating a very pleasing geometrical design on the floor of the nave. The frescoes were incredible, many of them floor to ceiling. Suzanne said it would take hours to really see one entire painting, and I'm sure she was right. Wonderful stone arches formed the side walls with the congregational seating area in between. Beyond the arches was a passageway wherein were stationed various altars and interesting artifacts.

"You know," I said to Lyn, "I've often wondered how Catholics keep their minds on the sermon with so much to look at."

She nodded, obviously agreeing with me but having nothing to say on the subject.

Jules quietly joined us. She pointed to a sign near one of the arches. *Silenso,* it read.

"Sorry," I whispered.

Jules whispered back. "I love all the candles in a Catholic church. It's almost romantic."

I paused to think about that. I can't say I've ever thought of a church as being romantic, but I could certainly see the possibilities.

Suzanne pointed toward the front of the church. Or the back. I never have been sure which end of a church is the back and which is the front. Whichever it was, Diana and Christmas were walking towards the door we had entered. We followed as quietly as we could, joined by Lyn and Annie.

"That was nice," said Diana. "And no sign of Panzinni."

"Did anyone look in the confession booth?" Suzanne's witty reference was not lost on us.

"I'm hungry," said Jules.

"I guess it's a good time to have lunch." Diana pulled out the list again. "The inspector suggested we dine at la Botte Goia. He says it's a restaurant with a gift shop."

Suzanne was the first to respond. "Ooo, that sounds nice. Eating and shopping are two of my favorite pastimes."

The inspector was correct in his assessment. We loved the little combination of wine shop, cheese shop, gift shop and restaurant. I have no idea what I ate, but it was delicious. We all passed around forkfuls of food for one another to taste until it got to be rather circus-like and Diana urged us to stop. For some reason, Christmas thought that was funny, and anytime Christmas thinks something is funny, we can't help but join her. Completely forgetting our purpose in visiting the charming little town of Pistoia, we laughed and chatted until Diana suddenly looked at her diamond-studded bracelet watch to check the time. "Oh, no. We can't sit here all day. Let's see what's next on the list. Hmm.... *Ospedale del Ceppo*. It was a twelfth-century hospital for the poor."

"Sounds exciting." I denoted a bit of cynicism in Suzanne's tone.

Diana didn't look up from the list. "It's known now for its friezes and its architecture."

"Let's go to the zoo," Christmas suggested.

Diana looked astonished. "The zoo? In Italy?"

"Sure," replied Christmas. "They have a nice zoo. The waiter told me about it."

"But Christmas," said Jules, "let's don't waste our time on something we can see back in the States."

Christmas smiled. "They may have different animals. What if there are Italian animals, and we never get to see them because we didn't go to the zoo in Tuscany?"

After pondering that a few seconds, Diana said, "We can't go because the zoo isn't on the list."

"Well," I said, "if the police are doing a good job, they could follow us to the zoo. They're supposed to be keeping an eye on us at all times."

Looking straight at Christmas and me who happened to be standing side-by-side, Diana, very pleasantly, replied, "We are *not* going to the zoo."

For the next few minutes, if I'm not mistaken, Christmas considered mutiny. I know I did. But in the end, we decided against it. We had voted

Diana the leader and added to that, we had promised to follow Inspector Franco's instructions. Italian animals could be looked up on the internet anytime.

We didn't stay long at the twelfth-century hospital. It was a lovely building, but I had to agree with Lyn that she had seen so many buildings all over Italy she was ready to see something different.

"What's next?" Jules leaned on Diana's shoulder to read the list.

Diana almost sang, "Gardens!"

"Wonderful!" Everyone echoed my response in their own way. Christmas said, "Yippee."

We hurried off behind Diana like a family of hungry mice scurrying to a round of cheese. And we were not disappointed. Oh, the peace and serenity of a garden. Little stone paths veered here and there through beds of colorful blooming flowers leading to little oases with benches and sometimes a table or two. One lane was lined with extremely tall, thin green plants that looked to be some type of juniper reaching to the sky. The effect was striking. I felt like royalty approaching my throne.

By a peaceful little pond surrounded by a rose garden, we sat down to rest and reflect. For me, it was a wonderful place to meditate, to count my blessings. I glanced at each of my friends, and I knew they felt the same. We stayed there for some time. Just before we rose to continue our tour, I thanked God there were no gangsters to ruin our time in the garden.

After visiting the last site on Inspector Franco's list, another church, we stood in a circle and wondered what to do next. It seemed too early to leave. Jules had a great idea. "I suggest we go over to that little outdoor café across the plaza and have something to drink or some gelato." Later, we would wonder what would have happened if we hadn't stayed in town to have ice cream.

Chapter Nineteen

MY GELATO WAS DELICIOUS. It tasted a lot like my grandmother's home-made ice cream. Licking it gave me time to think. "I've been thinking..."

Christmas giggled.

I looked at her and smiled. "Yes, I have been thinking, and there's something about this whole mess that I don't understand."

Diana looked interested. "What's that?"

"Well, why would Panzinni follow us around when he now knows where we live and could rob us at the villa anytime he wants to?"

"Because," explained Suzanne, "he knows Giovanni is there now as well as Mario. That's the inspector's theory, anyway. He wants to rob us when there are no big strong men around."

"I guess we'll have to admit that a police guard could be a bit intimidating," I replied.

"Giovanni wouldn't intimidate my dummy, Ken Chan," said Christmas.

Jules giggled. "I find myself hoping something will happen so I can see Giovanni in action. Isn't that terrible?"

Suzanne patted Jules's hand. "I know exactly what you mean. I just can't imagine that boy jumping around like Bruce Lee."

"I'm sure we would all be surprised," said Annie who had been extra quiet all day.

"Well, I've enjoyed this day even if it hasn't been as fruitful as Inspector Franco planned." I took one last lick of my gelato and wiped my hands.

"It has been nice," said Diana. "Pistoia is a lovely little town. I'm glad we came."

"Shouldn't we leave now?" Lyn held her purse in her lap. "I'd rather get back to the villa before dark."

"Yes," replied Diana. "It's time to go. Suzanne, since we all ordered the same thing, why don't you pay for the gelato out of the corporate purse?"

"Good idea."

"Now," said I, "where did we leave the van?"

Diana assured us she remembered the route we had taken. Being one who can't remember where she left her car in the mall parking lot, I was very impressed when the van appeared before our eyes. I think each of us must have breathed a sigh of relief. I know I did.

Being the smallest, Suzanne and Jules scrambled into the far back seats followed by Lyn, Diana and me in the middle row. Christmas got in on the passenger side while Annie removed the keys from her purse and placed her right foot on the running board. And that's when it happened.

Annie flew from the running board and landed on top of Christmas which caused Christmas to let out an unusually loud shriek. Before I could ask what on earth she was doing, a man jumped into the driver's seat and grabbed the keys from Annie's hand. In two jerks of a sheep's tail we were speeding out of Pistoia like a bat out of you-know-where. In retrospect, I think the shock paralyzed all of us. Except Annie, that is. She was struggling to untangle herself from Christmas. In the end, she sat almost upright in her old friend's lap, staring at what's-his-name Panzinni as if he were the devil himself.

I finally got my voice back. "Where are you taking us?"

My demand was met with a string of Italian that was so fast I didn't catch one word of it. And oddly enough, the man sounded as angry with me as he had in the airport restroom a lifetime ago. I was beginning to wonder if he had a thing against women which made him despise this particular assignment. I glanced at Diana, wondering if she had anything to say. She had those moon eyes again, and I think she tried to speak, but nothing came out.

Jules yelled from the back. "Do you speak English, signor Panzinni?"

He glanced in the rearview mirror and scowled; obviously surprised that Jules knew his name.

Lyn's body finally relaxed enough to lean over to whisper in my ear. "He'll kill us now that he knows we know his name, won't he?"

"No, Lyn, and you don't have to whisper. I found out in the airport restroom that the man doesn't know a word of English."

"But on TV they kill the hostages who can identify them."

"Listen, I will *not* die in Italy. Pete would never forgive me. Besides that, I have my memorial service planned to be held at home."

"Who is dead?" Both Jules and Suzanne had leaned up to hear more clearly. Diana seemed to be ignoring the unsettling conversation.

"Nobody is dead. Lyn was just sharing a few concerns."

"Like getting killed?" asked Suzanne.

"No one is getting killed," I assured them all. "If this man wanted to kill me, he could have done it any time within the past two weeks."

"Marn, you'll have to admit that this is the first time he's kidnapped you." Suzanne's tone was developing a little sarcasm.

I gave up. I always try to be an encourager, but I wasn't making a dent in my friends' understandable concerns. Since Panzinni couldn't speak English, I quickly decided the best thing to do for the time being was to ignore him. "Annie, can you tell where we're going? We left town so fast I didn't notice which road we took."

"No, I couldn't see then, and now I don't recognize the landscape. How about you, Christmas?" Annie tried to look back and down at Christmas but couldn't manage the turn.

"I can't see."

"Oh," said Annie.

Diana and I must have thought about the same thing at the same time again. We stared at one another until Diana whispered, "Do you see them?

"No, do you?"

"I'm afraid to look. Panzinni might notice, and then he would know the police are after him."

"That's true." I pondered that a few minutes. "Diana?"

"Yes?"

"Let's pray. He won't know a word we're saying. We need some angels."

"Great idea," said Diana with the first smile I'd seen since we left the gelato shop.

"Girls," said Diana, "we need to pray. He doesn't speak English, so we can pray for exactly what we need."

That seemed to bring the encouragement I was trying to give earlier which didn't surprise me one bit. It was a good thing because the van was taking curves at speeds I have never experienced. I wondered if Italy employed a highway patrol. If so, they were not doing a very good job.

Diana spoke up to get Annie's attention. "You pray, Annie, and we will agree with you."

"Me?" Annie didn't excel when put on the spot. She's one of those processing people who needs a little time to prepare. But Annie prayed that day. And being the one closest to our kidnapper, Panzinni heard every word even though he didn't understand it.

I wonder sometimes if prayer is not more for our sakes than for God's. That one was, for sure. More than likely, God had already put His plan in action and was just happy to be included. The main thing I noticed afterward was that no one seemed afraid. Nervous, yes, but not afraid.

We didn't see them coming, but all of a sudden, we heard them. Panzinni was talking on his cell phone, probably planning the venue for our imprisonment, when we first heard the siren. Frankly, I have never understood why law officers always use their sirens when they are pursuing a criminal. I mean, if you wanted to sneak up on me and catch me, would you blow a horn? But they did, and when Panzinni put the cell phone down, he heard it.

He must have been a crook for a long, long time because the sight of a red light blinking in the distance didn't seem to faze him one iota. He just took a deep breath and sped up. My greatest concern at that point was that the van would fall apart. The thing looked about my age to begin with, so I knew it couldn't handle the speediness. Panzinni didn't seem to share my concern.

Diana reached her hand back and tapped Suzanne's foot. "How close are they?"

She and Jules squirmed up to the edge of their seats again. "What did you say?"

"I asked if you can see how close they are?"

Jules boldly turned around to look out the back window. "I see the light blinking, but I can hardly see the vehicle."

"Oh, my goodness," said Lyn, her first words since the prayer.

Suddenly, I had an idea. "Jules, remember how you passed the truck that night and slowed him down by weaving back and forth in front of him?"

"Yes, and it would have worked if Mario hadn't come from the other direction. Why?"

"Well, if the police car could just catch up, that would be a good plan. Inspector Franco would eventually force Panzinni to stop."

"Well, he'd better get on up here."

Diana looked thoughtful. "I wonder why they are staying so far behind. Certainly, a police vehicle can go faster than this old van." She had a point.

"They're probably concerned he will kill us if they try anything," whispered Lyn.

This time I had no words of assurance. Her words rang true.

"What are they doing?" I whispered to Diana who was on my other side from Lyn.

"I don't know but I wish I did."

The inside of the van grew silent after that. I did notice that Jules turned to look behind us every now and then, but since she didn't give a report, I knew they were no closer, and that proved they were deliberately keeping their distance.

Annie gasped at the sight of something up ahead. At first, Panzinni lifted his right foot and pressed the brake pedal. It all happened so fast I'm not really sure about the sequence. Between Panzinni, Annie and Christmas, I could see very little out the front window, but what I did see looked like the roadblock I had seen in movies. My heart nearly jumped out of my chest. The other girls were on the edge of their seats. All I could think about was Annie. Considering her position, a head-on collision would likely kill her. I didn't think an extra prayer would hurt anything at that point.

Diana grabbed my hand and started softly but quickly praying in her own special way. Suzanne and Jules joined her. I glanced at Panzinni. He seemed to be making a decision as whether to run the road block or stop. He lifted his foot to place it back on the gas pedal. His decision was made.

And that's when our prayers were answered. Annie saw his foot move at the same moment I did. Instantly, she moved her own foot under his and blocked him from pressing the gas. It was like a Michael Jordan move on the basketball court. With her foot in the area, she pressed the brake, and before Panzinni could push her away, the van slowed down. Panzinni did his best to get Annie off him but her leg was entangled in his and neither of them could get free of the other. I pictured octopuses and other creatures with lots of appendages.

At the moment we saw the roadblock, the police vehicle had sped up fast enough to catch us, and when the van slowed down, Giovanni whipped the police car in front of the road block and stopped dead still, brakes squealing like a NASCAR pileup. I couldn't help but think that Pete would have enjoyed the scene if he had seen it on TV. That's when I saw a gun sticking out the back window of the police car and heard the sound of a tire exploding. For the next few minutes, I wondered if my memorial service would take place sooner than I had planned. And there I was on foreign soil with no one to attend. Maybe Pete would have my body shipped back to the States.

When our vehicle finally stopped spinning, the police invaded the van instantaneously. Panzinni had no chance to reach for his gun—if he had one—or grab Annie as his hostage which was something I had worried about earlier. He was in handcuffs before Mario and Giovanni opened the other doors to get us out.

Inspector Franco met a little difficulty in getting Panzinni's legs untangled from Annie's. We heard quite a bit of grunting and possibly cursing in Italian. Finally, Annie was free. She flopped over on Christmas and said, "Whew!"

We in the back seats watched the chaotic scene in stunned silence. It was one of those times when you want to do something to help but there is nothing to do and you couldn't do anything if there was because you are paralyzed. Mario, standing beside Diana's open door, waited patiently for us to move but no one did.

Just as the adrenalin slowed in its rush back and forth from my heart to my feet, Jules said, "You're our hero, Annie! Three cheers for Annie! Hip hip, hooray!"

We joined Jules but I have to tell you that our hoorays were just pitiful. Diana couldn't manage to get one out of her mouth. She sometimes has issues with her throat because of a thyroid condition but in this case, the problem was shock. Annie's eyes were still closed. She didn't seem too impressed with her heroics or anyone else's.

Lyn turned only her neck like that doll in the horror movie and whispered, "We're alive."

Chapter Twenty

TOO EXHAUSTED TO CELEBRATE yet too wound up to retire early that evening, my friends and I allowed Angelica and Pisa to fuss over us to their hearts' content. Lyn received a little extra attention because her stomach was still reeling from all that spinning.

I found her lying on the sofa in the living room. "How do you feel, Lyn?"

"Terrible. Remember when we used to go on those spinning rides at the state fair when we were teenagers? Well, I couldn't handle it then, and I can't now." She closed her eyes and waved me away.

Inspector Franco was in Florence interrogating Carlos Panzinni. Giovanni was with him learning the tools of the trade, I guess. Even Mario was absent. Where he was, I didn't know.

After Angelica stuffed us with a late breakfast, we took our coffee and tea cups and strolled down to the garden by the pool. Pisa happily pushed the serving cart behind us loaded with urns of coffee and hot water for tea along with pastries if we got hungry, which definitely would not happen any time soon.

The day was warm and vibrant. The late October sun played hide-and-go-seek with the whitest fluffiest clouds I've ever seen. The scent of autumn was in the air, my favorite time of the year. We were unusually quiet that fine morning. The sweet fragrance of Alberto's grapevines traveled slowly on the gentle breeze, delighting our sense of smell in the serenity of our own personal paradise.

Although our short-term memories couldn't help but revert back to scenes of yesterday, we found peace not only in our perfect surroundings but in being together. To have one good friend in life is a great gift. To have more is a special grace.

Jules stood up and looked around. "Do you hear music?"

"Sounds like signor Alberto's violin," replied Christmas. She, too, arose from the table and walked a ways down the path that led to Alberto's vineyard. In a few moments, we heard her call. "Come this way, girls."

Curious, we followed the sound of Christmas's voice to find her, and then we followed the sound of the violin. Christmas stopped us when we arrived at the edge of the largest vineyard on Alberto's property. The fragrance of the grapes was overpowering. It was almost as if we were drinking the juice through our noses. Christmas listened a few seconds to determine where the music was coming from and then led us down between two rows of vines. The sound of the violin slowly swelled as we grew closer to Alberto's location.

He didn't see us coming down the row, but we could see signor Alberto clearly. We stopped to watch and listen. The dear man was playing to the grapes and the vines. Later, he explained to Christmas that it was his harvest serenade, his last for the year. He believed his love for the land, given expression through the music, affected the vines and caused his grapes to make the best wine in Tuscany.

I don't know how long we stood there amid green vines and purple grapes receiving the music into our souls. Standing is often an activity that makes me very tired, but honestly, I didn't even think about it. We smiled and swayed with the sweet melodies until Alberto finally turned our way and caught us watching him way down the row. Staying true to his task, our Geppetto's eyes twinkled and his mustache twitched but he kept right on moving the bow across the strings, making sure that every single grape in the vineyard felt the love he expressed so tenderly. That was the first time I realized how handsome Alberto was but it obviously was not the first time for Christmas. She was glowing.

We were in awe. He smiled at us kindly, acknowledging our presence, but he did not stop playing. Slowly, he walked on to a new area of the vineyard, up and down the long rows, continuing his serenade of love.

We walked back to the garden in total silence, each of us pondering what we had seen. When we came to the pool, Jules's comment didn't break the sweet spell but added to it.

"He blessed the vineyard, didn't he? It was a blessing like in the Bible." Christmas spoke so softly we hardly heard her. "Yes . . . it was."

"I feel very blessed to have witnessed it," Diana said.

Suzanne was almost in tears. "You know, we've been in a lot of churches since we arrived in Italy, but that's the first time we've been *to* church."

There seemed nothing else to say.

⌒

Once again we gathered around the long dining table; this time wondering if Mario would be with us. Our answer came just as Diana started to look teary-eyed and Pisa brought in the *zuppa*. That beautiful man suddenly appeared in the archway looking as if he had received a blessing as well.

"Buona sera!" His wide smile bounced all over the room drawing smiles from each of us in return.

Diana looked like a flower in time-lapse photography. She was a tight little bud one moment, and suddenly, she was a radiant rose. Mario walked straight to her and leaned down to kiss her cheek. I was so glad they were getting over their embarrassment at showing their affection to one another. Or perhaps, I should say *passion*. That's a wonderful word, sometimes used incorrectly to imply actual physical actions. Not that there hadn't been any; I don't know, but true passion is an emotion of the heart which can be expressed in various ways or not at all. I was happy they were beginning to express theirs if only through a kiss on the cheek.

Loaded down with a large tray of antipasto, Angelica waddled into the room. Just before she sat the tray on the antique sideboard, she caught sight of the late dinner guest. What followed was, to us, totally unintelligible. She rattled off a tirade of Italian words that not even an Italian could have followed. Mario left his place beside Diana and went over to give Angelica a hug and all those kisses Italians deem necessary when greeting someone. I don't know what he said, but it sounded as if he tried to pacify her with a lot of excuses as to why he was so late and had caused her worry. I couldn't help but wonder why Angelica felt free to berate our guest. She hadn't treated us like that when we were late. I let it pass for the time being.

Finally, she calmed down and began to laugh, patting his back very motherly-like. Her plump little body shook merrily. It was then that I experienced a bit of vicarious *deja vous*. I had the feeling that this scene had been played many times over, ending the same way every time with Mario forgiven and Angelica placated. But that couldn't be true because we brought Mario with us, and Angelica didn't know him any better than she knew me and my friends. Of course, he was Italian and could speak her language so perhaps that explained it all.

Suzanne, who was sitting across from Mario, looked over at him and said, "We won't ask where you've been all day."

He got the point and laughed. "I have been taking care of business. Could you pass the ravioli, *per favore?*"

I hate to be nosey, and I'm usually not, but his reply did make me wonder. "I thought you were on vacation from the travel agent business."

Mario seemed more hungry than usual that evening. He ate a few bites of ravioli and Angelica's amazing garlic bread before he answered my question, though not to my satisfaction and not before he reached over to hold Diana's hand.

He gazed at her while he spoke to me. "There are many types of business, signora Marnie."

I do hate to be ignored, especially when I've asked a perfectly reasonable question. Suzanne had that familiar little squint in her eyes, letting me know she thought Mario was acting odd as well. Christmas looked pleasant as always. She must not have one nosey bone in her body. Lyn didn't care where Mario had been. It was all she could do to eat a few bites of bread. As for Jules, she paid us no mind. The vegetarian of our troop, she was loving the ravioli, the bread, the *insalata* and the white wine. I have always found it amazing how much that girl can eat and not gain weight.

I decided not to humiliate myself by continuing my line of questioning. Nevertheless, I did plan to speak with Diana later that night ... *if* she became available.

Diana rose as gracefully as a swan. "Why don't we have our coffee in the living room?"

"I'm going to bed." Lyn looked as if she might not make it up the stairs.

"We understand, darlin," Jules assured her. "Hope you feel better tomorrow."

Once again each of us migrated to our preferred seats and wiggled and squirmed until we were as comfortable as possible, except for Diana. She took her place beside Mario like a queen joining her consort. He reached for her hand.

"Have you heard from Inspector Franco today, Mario?" Jules drew her knees to her chest and rested her chin on top, an admirable feat, I must say.

"He called around noon to tell me the interrogation was over."

"Well?" Diana looked up at him. "What did he find out?"

"Not as much as he would have liked. Panzinni admitted to the burglary here in the villa as well as to following you for the past two weeks. But he refused to name his boss or any of his superiors in the syndicate."

"How about kidnapping? Did he admit to that?" Suzanne asked.

Mario laughed. "He said he asked if he could borrow the van and you gave him permission."

"What?" Jules nearly screamed which is what I wanted to do.

"I can't believe it." Annie shook her head.

"Don't worry. The inspector and Giovanni, me and the other officers involved, we can testify to his guilt along with all of you. Kidnapping is a serious charge in Italy."

I was incensed. "As well it should be. That man is a crook!"

Christmas laughed. "We know that, Marnie."

"You know what I mean. Carlos Panzinni is a mean man, and I wish I had never laid eyes on him."

"Don't we all," said Diana.

Mario tried to be covert about it, but I saw that he slowly lifted the hand that wasn't holding Diana's and draped his arm on the back of the sofa behind her. As I watched, he carefully and even more slowly, eased his arm down until it was draped around her shoulders. She looked at her lovely manicure and smiled.

"What happens next?" Suzanne asked.

"He will go to trial when the prosecution is ready."

Annie asked the question, but it was mine as well. "They won't let him out of jail, will they?"

"No, they will not. Franco said that if it were a case of minor burglary, he might be released on bail. But with the kidnapping charge, Panzinni will be kept behind bars until his trial. If convicted, he will put in prison for a very long time."

"*If?*" Jules asked.

"I am sure he will be convicted," said Mario, "but Franco said that when a case involves a syndicate as large as this one, the *avvocato* sometimes gets the criminal released." He glanced down at Diana. "What is it called in English?"

"Lawyer?"

"Si, the crime syndicates have their own lawyers who are very experienced in finding little, ah . . . holes in the prosecution's strategy."

"Well," I said, "we'll just have to pray about that."

Jules stood up and stretched. Yawning, she sat back down and laid her head on Christmas's shoulder. "I suggest we change the subject and talk about something fun before I go to bed."

Christmas spoke up. "signor Alberto asked me to invite you all to the grape harvest festival at his villa tomorrow evening. They will be picking all day, and you can help with that if you'd like. I'm going to. There will be a big outdoor dinner, and all Alberto's family and friends and neighbors will be there. He really wants us to go."

"Oh, that will be wonderful," I replied. "I'd love to go."

"Yay, we're going to have fun!" Jules got up and danced around the room, happy as a lark in springtime. "Come on, Suzanne, dance with me."

"You dance, and I'll watch. I need to save my energy for grape picking."

I couldn't have agreed more. "I'm going to bed. Tomorrow will be a busy day. *Buona sera,* everybody."

"Come to bed, Jules. We can dance tomorrow." Suzanne yawned and stretched.

Diana and Mario were left alone in the gathering room while we climbed the stairs for bed. My last glance at the lovers from the balcony was well worth the look. Mario pulled Diana close to himself and gently lifted her face to his. I don't know how long they gazed into each other's eyes, but what came next was the purest sweetest kiss I have ever been allowed to witness—a kiss that made a tear roll down my own cheek.

Chapter Twenty-one

HARVEST DAY DAWNED BRIGHT AND CLEAR. Roosters crowed and birds sang. I made a mental note to ask Christmas the name of the birds who so cheerfully woke me up every morning we stayed at the villa. I wanted to take them home with me. They reminded me of a similar morning in my childhood when my grandmother said to my grandfather, "I just love those singing birds." My grandfather said to my grandmother, "If I had a gun, I'd shoot 'em."

Weeks earlier, we had agreed that the one thing we would *not* do on vacation was rush. Of course, with the Mafia on our trail, we had been forced to hurry a few times, but that was not in the original plan. We had promised one another to enjoy sweet, lazy mornings and to schedule absolutely nothing before ten. We had also promised to give one another space when needed. There was no reason that seven mature women had to be together every hour of the day and night like a bunch of teenagers. And so it was that the morning of the harvest festival, I arose with a strong need for some time alone.

When Suzanne passed my door, I called her in. "Do you mind asking Pisa to bring a tray to my room? I think I'm going to write some postcards and perhaps do a little bit of nothing before the day becomes so busy."

"Sure. Wish I'd thought of that myself."

It seemed only minutes before Pisa arrived with a lovely silver tray adorned with a tantalizing breakfast and a small vase of bright pink roses in the center. I felt like a princess in my tower. I asked her to set the tray outside on the balcony. I settled down in a comfortable plushy chair, nibbling from the tray, listening to the birds and writing a few words every now and then. If there is a Seventh Heaven, I had a little taste of it that morning.

I was sipping my coffee when I heard light steps through the open doors to my room. I closed the front of my cotton robe and tied the sash, wondering who it might be. Diana's smiling face peeped around the doorway.

"Well, how nice!"

"Do you mind? I know you're enjoying this time by yourself, but I would like to chat with you a few minutes if it's okay."

"Sure. What a delightful surprise. We haven't had much time to talk."

Diana sat in the chair on the other side of the small table. She was beautifully groomed and all ready for the day. Her Murano glass necklace flickered in the morning sun. Looking out over the gardens below, my friend sighed deeply, breathing in the fragrance of the roses that wafted up to fill our senses with such sweet pleasure. It was quite a while before she spoke again, and when she did, her voice was very soft and low.

"Marnie, I want to stay here."

"So do I." I smiled and sipped my coffee.

"I know we all want to stay because we love it so, but that's not what I meant. I *really* want to stay. As a matter of fact, I'm going to stay."

I stared at her, studying the seriousness of what she had said as well as sensing the turmoil she had gone through to get to this place.

"You know . . . I'm not surprised, not really. Mario, I presume?"

"Yes. He asked me to marry him last night."

I will forever remember the glow that emanated from Diana's lovely face that beautiful morning in Tuscany. My friend had found love, and she was determined not to let it slip away.

"Oh, Diana, I'm so happy for you." I tried to get out of the chair to hug her, but with a lap filled with postcards, my journal and writing pens, it was too much of a struggle.

"Don't get up." She got up and stepped over to hug me instead.

"Oh, my!" I exclaimed. "This means we will be coming back for the wedding, right?"

"Hmm . . . maybe." I could tell Diana was teasing me. She obviously had more to tell than she was telling.

"Yeeeeessss?"

"We wanted to have the wedding tonight at the harvest festival."

"Oh, my goodness!"

Diana laughed at my reaction and squeezed my hand. "Can you believe it? I can't. I keep pinching myself."

"No! Have you told the others? They are going to faint!"

"Just Annie, and she's very happy for me."

"Well, for a while there, I thought she might strike something up with Inspector Franco, but it seems she's not too interested."

"You know Annie. She would never be willing to leave her grandchildren."

"That's true."

"I'm going to go down and tell the others now. Oh, there's one more thing." Diana stepped back to her chair and sat down. "Marnie, you will never believe this in a thousand years."

"What on earth?"

"Mario owns this villa."

"What?!"

"He does."

"That means that you're going to get to live in this paradise the rest of your mortal life?"

She grinned and placed her palm on her forehead. "Ohhh, my head! I feel like I'm still spinning in the van at the roadblock."

"Pete says that anything too good to be true is exactly that, too good to be true. There's got to be a catch in all this somewhere."

"Nope, no problems unless you call getting our marriage license a problem. That's why we can't have the wedding tonight. We've applied, but since I'm an American, the process takes a little longer. And anyway, I want my mom and dad to be here."

I looked out at the gardens and the rolling hills mapped by vineyards as far as my eyes could see. "Oh, my goodness," I murmured. "You will be the queen of the castle, Diana." And then I thought out loud, "How often can we visit?"

She laughed. "As often as you possibly can. Mario adores you all."

"Hmm, now I understand the strange scene with Mario and Angelica yesterday morning. She and Pisa are his employees." I was amazed at all the intrigue involved in something as simple as a little vacation.

"Yes. He thought you picked up on that."

My thinking cap was working overtime. "And that's why he knew about the horses and the golf carts and all that stuff."

Diana laughed as she rose once more. "Yes. You should have been a PI, Marnie. You're the best Sherlock Holmes I know." She made a move towards the door. "I'd better go. I need to talk to the others, and then Mario and I are going to drive into Florence. I need a few things, and Mario has very good taste."

"I've noticed . . . Diana?"

She had stepped through the open doors. "Yes?"

"Is Mario really a travel agent and tour guide?"

My question drew another round of laughter from the friend who has always been very careful with expressions of emotion. "Yes, he is a travel agent. He has offices all over Europe, in fact."

"Oh, no wonder he can afford this place."

"Marn, I have another secret. It's about signor Alberto."

"Come back this instant and sit down."

Diana obeyed me for once. "Remember all the times we've been over to signor Alberto's land? We had the picnic by the lake, and then we visited the vineyards yesterday and heard him playing the violin?"

I was nodding at every reminder. "And . . . ?"

"It isn't signor Alberto's land. It belongs to Mario and your Geppetto is his overseer."

"Oh, my goodness." I almost gasped when I thought of it. "So Mario is the husbandman!"

I had never seen Diana laugh so much unless it was in one of our corporate giggling sessions. "Yes and I will be the wife of the husbandman."

We both laughed at that. What joy it was to be happy for a friend.

⌒

After Diana left, I went over everything she had said, enjoying every minute, for a very long time. And at some point in the midst of my musings I did something I've never done in my life. At ten in the morning, on the balcony of a villa in Tuscany still in my robe, I drifted off to sleep.

Only the gong of the lunch bell woke me up and then I again remembered that Angelica doesn't ring the lunch bell. I wondered what was going on, but I was still in my robe so I gathered up my writing paraphernalia and ignored the bell to take a shower and ready myself for the harvest festival. As one who is not prone to a lot of primping, it didn't take very long.

As I walked down the stairs, the villa seemed totally empty. It was a rather odd feeling to be in such a large house alone. I couldn't help but wonder who was going to drive my golf cart. I got to the kitchen as Angelica's behind was going out the back door. Thankfully, Lyn was just in front of her because she could drive the cart. Lyn can drive anything from a tractor to a bulldozer. I called for her to wait.

"Where have you been?" she asked. "Didn't you hear the bell?"

"Yes, but I thought it was a mistake since it doesn't ring for lunch. Why?"

"We were to meet at the garage when the bell rang so that we could all go over to Alberto's together." Angelica was nodding as if she understood what Lyn was saying.

"Oh, I must have missed the instructions. Why are you still here?"

Lyn looked exasperated. "I was waiting for you, but when you never came down, I decided I might as well go over to Alberto's with Angelica."

I smiled. "That was nice of you. Do we have to walk?" I nearly groaned.

"No, I'd rather not drive because my head is still spinning a little but Angelica can drive. She does it all the time."

"How do you know?"

"Christmas told me. She understands everything."

I grabbed my shoulder bag and followed Lyn out the door to the garage. Angelica chattered all the way.

Pete has what I consider a very large extended family. Normally, fifty people or so show up at Aunt Millie's house for Thanksgiving and at ours on off years. However, our fifty family members were a drop in the bucket compared to the multitudes I saw when we arrived at the edge of the vineyard behind Alberto's villa. I thought to myself that only Suzanne had more cousins than Alberto. Many of the guests were, of course, friends and neighbors, but the overwhelming majority was family belonging to Mario as well as Alberto. That's when we discovered another surprising fact.

Lyn and I quickly joined our friends while Angelica shuffled off to help with the food. Mario began to introduce us to everybody one at a time, and then he quickly realized that that would take all night and the following day. Finally, Alberto motioned for Mario to step up on the platform which had been erected for the musicians who were happily playing their hearts out. Alberto held his hand up to signal the little band to pipe down for a few minutes.

This time the amazing smile on our Italian hunk's face blessed a multitude. He reached down to pull signor Alberto up to stand beside him. I couldn't help but notice a slight resemblance. *Mario might look like Geppetto, too, when he gets a little older,* I thought.

"*I miei amici.*" He began his speech by calling us friends and then addressed his family as well, "*La mia famiglia.*" Mario looked around, smiling at everyone. It took quite a while because he had to translate as he went along, but the man I then knew was our host first welcomed all his guests and then placed his arm around signor Alberto's shoulders. That's when we found out Alberto was his uncle, his favorite *zio,* as well as the overseer of his vineyards.

I caught Diana's eye with a question in mine. She just smiled impishly and turned away, moving a little closer to the platform. Together, Mario and Alberto thanked their employees for a prosperous year of hard work and commitment. I couldn't understand Italian but it was easy to see that one man picked up where the other left off. It was also easy to see that nephew and uncle shared the relationship of father and son or perhaps older brother to adoring younger. They were family and it was beautiful to see.

Mario smiled down at Diana and reached out his hand. Our gracious Diana stepped up to take her place between Mario and signor Alberto. I tell you, she was a sight to behold. Our dear sister, happier than she had ever been in her life, wore a soft buttery yellow sundress that flowed this way and that in the gentle breeze. I loved her hat. Wide brimmed and a little flimsy, the matching hat set off her blue eyes to perfection. No wonder Mario couldn't take his eyes off her.

Mario continued his address first in Italian and then in English.

"Today, I take great pleasure in introducing you to *il mio* fiancée, Diana."

Except for six smiling American women, the crowd was stunned. I couldn't help but think that if Mario's mother had been living, she would have fainted straightaway. Angelica, probably the closest thing to a mother, looked as if she might have a heart attack. I have no idea what she was saying and more than likely, I wouldn't want to know, but during her outburst, she frantically fanned her face with a magazine and wiped tears away with the other hand. Poor thing, he should have told her ahead of time in my opinion.

While Mario and Diana happily gazed into one another's eyes, the shock finally wore off enough for the majority of the multitude to accept the news with great joy. Suddenly, cheers and applause were running rampant throughout the land, and the newly engaged couple turned to face their audience once again. This time, Diana, ever so regally, extended her left hand for all to see. And this time her closest friends were included in those shocked. I tell you, that rock must have weighed a half pound. Later, Annie told us it was three carats.

Suzanne made the only remark in response. "Our Diana has hit the jackpot."

"Congratulazioni! Congratulazioni!" The crowd yelled and cheered until Mario must have decided the only way he was going to get to eat was to help Diana off the platform and walk towards the banquet table. He placed his right hand at Diana's lower back, prodding her tenderly towards the spectacular feast.

My friends and I hardly spoke to Diana the remainder of the evening. Her soft yellow dress of varying lengths flowed continuously throughout the gathering, gently guided by the love of her life. Admiring eyes followed the couple everywhere they went, including mine.

Oh, my goodness, we ate until I thought I would be sick. Even Lyn tasted most everything on the table and didn't gag the first time. I don't know what it is about Italian food. I seriously doubt there is one item on a menu in Italy that I wouldn't like. And if they borrowed their pasta from the Chinese, I for one, am glad. China is much too far away.

Just as the sun went down over the Tuscan hills and candles began to flicker all about, Christmas stepped up on the low platform, guitar in hand. She sat on a stool while Alberto stood beside her with his violin and together they made music the likes of which I've never heard before. I don't know if it was Italian or American or in between, but it was soft and sweet and beautiful. Every now and then they looked at one another and smiled, Alberto's mustache twitching happily.

Jules leaned close and whispered. "Another wedding ya think?"

I shrugged. "Who knows? They sure do seem to fit, don't they?"

She nodded. "They look great together, as perfect as Mario and Diana .... Marn?"

"Uh, huh?" I was in dreamland, planning weddings this way and that.

"This has been the strangest vacation, don't you think?" Jules put her arm around my waist.

"Yes, I do think. Never in a million years did I dream we would encounter a gangster or that it would end like this with Diana getting married and Christmas obviously deep in some type of relationship."

Jules sighed. "I think I'll dance," She turned to her left. "Time to dance, Suzanne."

Suzanne clearly agreed, and off they went towards the area created for a dance floor in front of the platform. All cheerful and excited, our two youngest sisters joined our friends in the limelight. They twirled and swirled to their hearts content. The Italians were delighted as well as Alberto and Christmas. People began to join them, young and old alike. From small children to more Geppettos and even a few Sophia Lorens, nearly everyone danced. That night I decided that Italian women are just as beautiful as Italian men. Subsequently, I couldn't help but wish my Gaelic ancestors had passed down a few Italian genes, but I guess that wasn't possible.

My sisters and I, the five left out of the romance scene, parked ourselves in very comfortable lawn chairs and slowly sipped our red wine, the Beaujolais of the Italian grape harvest. My middle granddaughter always wanted to be the watcher at any event, family or otherwise, and that night at the harvest festival I wholeheartedly concurred. We had front row seats at the party of the century.

Mario and Diana must have wandered off alone a few times because I was keeping a pretty close watch on the lovers, and even then, I lost track of them a time or two. I did notice that each time they showed up, they looked a great deal happier than before they left.

"Mar?" Suzanne always calls me Mar. "Have you seen anyone stomping grapes?"

"No, but I missed the picking and all that. The stomping part could have been earlier."

Suzanne shook her head. "I picked a couple of hours with Jules and Christmas and never saw the first person stomp a grape."

"I thought they dumped all the grapes in a huge vat and everyone jumped in and started stomping, like Lucy and Ethel."

"I did, too, and to tell you the truth, I was looking forward to it."

Jules joined in from the other side of Suzanne. "I could hardly wait. I was planning on dancing on the grapes."

We stared at Jules for a few seconds before she burst out laughing. I had no idea it was a joke. I could easily imagine her dancing on grapes.

"Was the picking fun?" I love to hear reports of everyone's activities.

"Yeah," replied Jules, "but it was work, that's for sure."

Suzanne nodded. "We were given pretty baskets and little scissors and told not to pick any grapes that were bruised or molded. After our baskets were filled, we carefully emptied them into a thing that looked like the back of a dump truck."

"Oh, the grapes smelled sooooo good," said Jules.

"Everything smells good in Italy," I said, taking a deep breath. "Food, grapes, wine, flowers, Mario—everything."

Around ten o'clock, right out of the blue, I got this terrible longing in my heart to see Pete. That's when I knew it was time to go home; we had been apart long enough. Napoli and the sea would have to wait until another day. Home was at the top of my itinerary, and Pete was waiting.

Chapter Twenty-two

WE ALL SLEPT LATE the day following the harvest festival, our final day in Tuscany. To tell you the truth, I think we were all ready to head home. Everyone except Diana.

I had a few questions I didn't want to leave unanswered. "Aren't you even going to go back for your personal items and your household effects?"

"Not now," Diana replied. "Nothing is more important than being with Mario."

I wondered if one's spirit can literally glow outside one's body. If so, Diana's did. It was like the halo you see in religious paintings except that it glowed all the way down rather than just around her head. Every one of my friends saw it and told me so on the plane during the long flight home.

Lyn was beside herself, bubblier than Suzanne when she gets wired up. She talked a blue streak all morning. I even heard her muttering alone in her room when I passed by the door. I did hope nothing would happen to Pops before Lyn got home because she would never have forgiven herself.

Each of us spent the morning packing and repacking according to the amount of shopping we had done. It took all morning, even with Pisa's unwavering help. Angelica was cooking our last meal, crying as if it were really our last meal. We met in the dining room one last time, and guess who came for dinner, or lunch, as it were? Inspector Franco was seated in the middle of the long table laden down with the very best of Angelica's repertoire. He was ready with loads of apologies that he had missed the harvest festival. It was obvious the poor man was telling the truth, not just offering excuses.

A smiling Giovanni sat between Inspector Franco and Annie. One of

Franco's reasons for missing the festival satisfied us right off the bat. The dear man had stayed late at the office working on the case just so we would be free to take our scheduled flight back to North Carolina. Each of us expressed our thanks and appreciation for his kindness, and Jules even jumped up and ran around the table to give him a hug. He was visibly thrilled.

Signor Alberto arrived just as Jules took her seat again. Amid happy faces and cheerful welcomes, that sweet man walked around the table and did that Italian kissing thing to each of us, one at a time. Mario explained that he was saying goodbye before we left for the airport. Harvest issues would keep him from going with us to Rome. When he got to Christmas, I don't know whose face was redder, hers or his. After dodging heads a time or two, he took her hand in his and kissed it tenderly. This time I wished Pete had inherited a few Italian genes.

I addressed Inspector Franco who happened to be sitting across from me. "So. We're free to leave Italy, Inspector?"

"Si, si, signora. Your testimonies have been recorded with the court, and everything is in order. The court has been very gracious to you, my friends. Because Giovanni took photographs of each of you to be documented with my reports, the judge believes you will not be needed at Panzinni's trial. However, if an emergency comes up, we may have to call you back to Italy."

"Yippee!" Christmas clapped her hands and stole a sly glance at Alberto for which she received a few twitches of his mustache in return as well as a twinkle in his eye.

Laughter is definitely contagious, and it certainly was that day. We laughed and talked and listened to one another for over an hour; even Lyn joined in. No one said it aloud, but we were obviously looking forward to the fact that some unforeseen difficulty would arise in Panzinni's court case that would give us the opportunity to fly back to Italy and visit Diana and Mario. Perhaps we might finally get to tour Napoli and Sicily as well which were included in our original itinerary. My mind was speeding faster than Panzinni had driven the van that infamous day in the Tuscan countryside.

"Are you going with us to the airport, Inspector?" Annie looked as if she wanted him to go, but then again, I wasn't sure. Annie was hard to read sometimes.

"No, signora, I wish it were possible, but it is not. Giovanni and I have been assigned a new case, and we must be diligent."

Annie looked at Giovanni and smiled. "Don't forget the things we've talked about."

"I will not forget. And I will never forget you, signora." We never did get to see him use his black belt.

The inspector stood, and Giovanni rose with him. "We have one more thing to do before we can let you go," said the inspector.

Lyn gasped aloud and then clamped her hand over her mouth. We stared at Franco like Annie had at Panzinni that day in the van, like he was the devil himself.

"No, no. There is no problem in your case," said Inspector Franco. Giovanni grinned, joined by Mario. Something was up, and I could see that even Diana didn't know about it. Giovanni leaned down to get something from under his chair.

"Signora," Franco began, turning to Annie. "You have been awarded an honorary citation from the Firenze police department."

Mario and Giovanni grinned. Annie's jaw dropped an inch at least. That much of an emotional response from Annie was just short of a miracle.

"Annie," said the inspector, rather tenderly, I thought, "had you not fought to place your foot on that brake, I do not know where you would be today. I am sure your friends owe their lives to you. We are also certain in Firenze, that we owe you great honor and respect as well as many thanks for capturing this notorious criminal. Panzinni was a wanted man as you say in America, and you, my friend, were responsible for his capture. We thank you."

Giovanni walked around the long table and after handing her the plaque, he kissed her on both cheeks. She pulled him close and wrapped her arms around him. "I always hug my boys," she said.

The plan was for Mario and Diana to drive us to Rome to meet our plane. I think we were all happy to get a night flight. Sleeping takes up a lot of

worrying time when one is flying at four thousand feet over the Atlantic
Ocean and could take a dive any minute. The only stop would be in the
village for Suzanne to drop off her watercolors. There hadn't been time to
go back to the village but Mario had taken care of the arrangements and
the proprietor of the little shop was eagerly awaiting Suzanne's work.

Mario had traded in our poor, worn out van for a much newer, sporti-
er version for our riding pleasure. The van was waiting at the door. Those
little Italian boys Mario seemed to always have at his beck and call scattered
about the villa gathering our luggage and extra bags and anything else that
needed to go home with us. For a little while, our enchanted garden was
overtaken with erratic noise and activity that seemed quite foreign compared with the peace and tranquility of its former days. The boys ran in
and out while Pisa and Angelica gave them orders that seemed to go on
and on and on. And then, suddenly, all was quiet.

The seven of us plus Mario, Angelica, Pisa and Alberto stood by the
waiting van. It was quite apparent that no one wanted to get in. Naturally,
it took some time to pull ourselves away from Angelica and Pisa. They had
fallen in love with us and us with them. One of the ways Angelica showed
her love was to stuff us with her wonderful food. She had packed enough
for us to gain ten pounds each on the way home.

It seems now that all the chatter stopped instantaneously. We stood in
silence, waiting for someone to move first. It was a little odd that Annie
was the one who broke the stillness.

"Change of plans, girls," she said. "I don't know about you all, but I
want my last memory of Diana and our new friends to be here in our
enchanted garden, not in an impersonal place like an airport."

"Annie, you're the wisest woman I know," said I. "That's a great idea."

The smile that flowed from one to the other was a good indication of
unanimous agreement. To tell the truth, a heavy weight seemed to lift right
off my shoulders. I turned to Christmas who was flirting with Alberto and
whispered, "Fess up, girlfriend. What's happening with you two?"

"Later," she whispered back.

I suddenly remembered that I had one thing to get straight before we
said goodbye. "Diana?"

"Hmm?" I was surprised to see her lean on Mario's shoulder.

"Have you set the date?" I knew the others wanted to know as well.

"Not yet, but we're thinking about Christmas."

"You can't get married during Christmas," said Annie in a most matter of fact tone.

"And why not?" Diana turned around to face us.

My eyebrows rose involuntarily as I stared at her. "Well, I for one couldn't come."

"Neither could I," said Suzanne. "My four children and their families, mom and dad, cousins and more cousins—they all come to my house. Christmas is family time."

"I can come, Diana," said Christmas, glancing Alberto's way. "My sisters wouldn't mind."

"Thank you, Christmas," replied Diana.

Lyn refused to join the conversation, I could tell. Getting her away from Pops again would be more of a miracle than I had faith to believe for.

Mario just smiled.

"I'll be in New York with my daughter this Christmas," said Jules, her face filled with disappointment.

"Would you girls like to set the date for our wedding?" Diana laughed. She smiled at each of us, and I knew she was thinking how much she would miss us in the weeks and years ahead.

"That's up to you and Mario," I said.

Diana raised her eyebrows and smiled. "Oh, *really?*"

"Yes, but please remember that your friends will have to fly across the ocean to get to your wedding, and time is of the essence as well as money."

"Yeah," said Jules, "we're not rich."

"Not yet," said Christmas. I think I noticed Alberto's twinkle in her eye.

My one concern was leaving Diana in a foreign land for the rest of her life with a man—even though he *was* a hunk—she had known only a few weeks. What if they had a falling out and she had no one to lean on, no one to help her get back home in her heartbroken state? What if she found out Mario was a bigamist? Or what if his grown children hated her? This time I was forced to shake my head to get rid of the pictures.

I saw Mario squeeze Diana's hand, not the one with the rock. Before I could figure out how to verbalize my concerns without offending anyone, Jules did it for me.

"Diana, darlin', are you sure it's best for you to stay in Italy now? Don't you have things to wrap up at home?"

Our friend smiled at us as if she were Snow White and we were the Seven Dwarfs. I half expected her to pat our heads. "No." Her voice was soft and tender. She looked up at Prince Charming and glowed like the morning sun. "My life is here now."

Angelica and Pisa ran back into the house, Angelica chattering away between sobs and Pisa wiping tears from her eyes. We stood in a circle there in the driveway looking, I'm sure, like seven grieving women, one very happy Italian hunk and a kindhearted Geppetto who was quite handsome in his own right. However, positive thinking always wins the day. The thought of Diana and Mario together forever touched our hearts and lifted our spirits for the long journey home.

Diana pulled Annie close and then each of us took our turn. We were leaving our friend on a vacation of all things. Lyn said later she felt as if Diana got lost and we went home without her. Annie said, "She isn't lost. She's found."

It was time for me to say something to Mario I'd had on my heart. "Well, Mario Daniele. We were all hoping for a Divine appointment in Italy, and guess what? You were it. How does it feel to be a Divine appointment?"

I'll have to say that Mario looked a bit shaken. Diana linked her arm in his.

"I am overwhelmed," he said, his wonderful smile nowhere to be seen. "I am honored, *i miei amici.*"

"We have the honor," said Jules. "You have been so good to us, not the other way around. At first I thought you were a male chauvinist pig but you turned out okay."

Mario laughed and gave Jules a hug. "I can never repay you, my friends. You brought me my Diana."

That incredible smile appeared once again. I'm sure each of us was convinced there was no way to top that. We continued to stand there in the circle, smiling at one another like the old Hit Parade song, "Mutual

Admiration Society."

I almost stumbled towards the van, thinking how much I would miss this beautiful country as well as my old friend and my new ones. I started counting new friends with each step—Mario, signor Alberto, Inspector Franco, Angelica, Pisa, Giovanni, the guy at the little country pit stop, the Englishman in the restroom, cousins and more cousins . . . . And then we all turned around for the last time and blew Diana kisses until we nearly tripped over each other's feet.

I was almost in the van when I caught a glimpse of Christmas out of the corner of my eye. She and signor Alberto were holding hands, smiling into each other's eyes. The scene was so sweet I almost cried. I wondered if two of our seven might be calling Italy home before long.

I tell you, it was like pulling eye teeth to get us away from our enchanted garden and our dear friends. Finally, with tears in all our eyes, Annie pulled the van away and turned it around to head down the long driveway to the highway. If I remember correctly, we were all sniffling and wiping tears from our eyes. That is, until Christmas stuck her head out the window and shouted, "Arrivederci, y'all!" That broke us up.

CPSIA information can be obtained at www.ICGtesting.com
Printed in the USA
LVOW061010180911

246781LV00004B/181/P

9 780980 019698

ML

10/11